MW01031690

ALSO BY RIKKI DUCORNET

The Stain
Entering Fire
The Fountains of Neptune
The Cult of Seizure
The Jade Cabinet
The Complete Butcher's Tales
Phosphor in Dreamland
The Word "Desire"
The Fan-Maker's Inquisition
The Monstrous and the Marvelous

GAZELLE

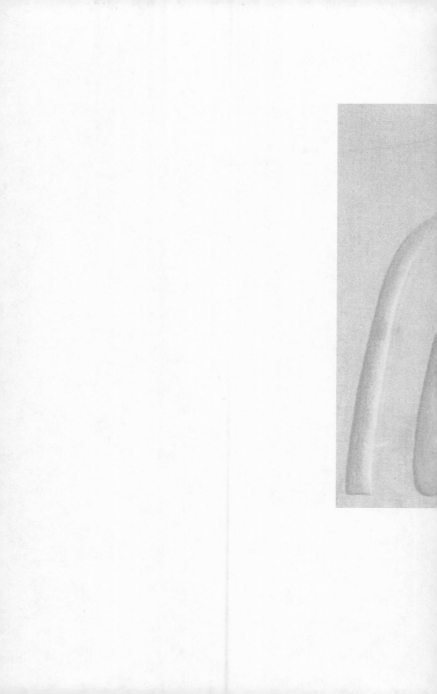

GAZELLE

A novel

Rikki Ducornet

ALFRED A. KNOPF   NEW YORK   2003

THIS IS A BORZOI BOOK
PUBLISHED BY ALFRED A. KNOPF

Copyright © 2003 by Rikki Ducornet

All rights reserved under International and Pan-American Copyright
Conventions. Published in the United States by Alfred A. Knopf,
a division of Random House, Inc., New York, and simultaneously
in Canada by Random House of Canada, Limited, Toronto.
Distributed by Random House, Inc., New York.

www.aaknopf.com

Knopf, Borzoi Books, and the colophon are registered trademarks
of Random House, Inc.

Chapter one was previously published in *The Word "Desire,"*
Henry Holt, 1994.

Quotes from the mother's book are taken from *Glorify Yourself*
by Eleanor King, Prentice Hall, 1952 (tenth printing).

Library of Congress Cataloging-in-Publication Data

Ducornet, Rikki, [date]
Gazelle / Rikki Ducornet.—1st ed.
p. cm.
ISBN 0-375-41124-0 (alk. paper)
1. Americans—Egypt—Fiction.   2. Perfumes industry—Fiction.
3. Cairo (Egypt)—Fiction.   4. Teenage girls—Fiction.   I. Title.

PS3554.U279 G3 2003
813'.54—dc21   2002034000

Manufactured in the United States of America
First Edition

For Kai and Elina

I question travellers
from the four corners of the earth
hoping to meet one
who has breathed your fragrance.

—Abū Bakr al-Turtūshī

Contents

GAZELLE

ONE

The Chess Set of Ivory

Chess appealed to my father's delight in quietude, his repressed rage, his trust in institutions, models, and measured behavior. Chess justified what Father liked best: thinking about thinking. He called it: *battling mind.*

Father dwelled in a space of such disembodied quietness his Egyptian students called him His Airship, I believe with affection. Chess allowed Father to make decisions that would in no way influence the greater world—beyond his grasp anyway—and to engage in conflict without doing violence to others or to himself. (Father's fear of thuggery suggested clairvoyance when in a later decade he would find himself undone by a handful of classroom Maoists who called him Gasbag to his face. If clearly they intended to hurt him, they were, admittedly, responding to that disembodied quality of his already evident in Egypt, and to his pedantry—a quality rooted in timidity.)

Father was a closet warrior, a mild man and an intellectual, a dreamer of reason in a world he feared was chronically, terminally unreasonable. And he was a parsimonious conversationalist. His favorite quote was from Wittgenstein: "What we cannot speak of we must be silent about." When Father did speak, he spoke so softly that even those who knew him well had to ask him to repeat himself. Once, during his Fulbright year in Egypt, when several of his students had discovered a crate of brass hearing trumpets for sale in the bazaar, they had carried these to class to—at a prearranged signal—lift them simultaneously to their ears. (Yet, in sleep, Father ground his teeth so loudly my mother nightly dreamed of industry: gravel pits, cement factories, brickworks.)

I could add that Father was fastidious, sometimes changing his clothes two or three times a day. He ate little and dressed soberly—if with a specific, outdated flair: on formal occasions he wore a cummerbund. I took after him, played quietly by myself behind closed doors. And if Mother—and she was a big, beautiful Icelander—was a noisemaker, she made her noise out in the world—the Officers Club, for example.

Father once admitted to me that chess saved him from losing his mind—and this was said after he had lost his heart. When he played he became disembodied—a mind on a stalk in a chair, invisible—and if he could keep ahead of his adversary, impalpable, too. In life as in chess, Father did not want to be touched, to be moved, to be seized; he was unwilling to be pinned down or cornered. He jumped from one discourse to another, embracing peculiar and obscure concepts and ideologies about which no one else knew anything; meaningful conversation with him proved an impossibility. In those years chess became the sole vehicle by which he could be reached, or rather, *engaged*—for he could never be reached—the navigable airspace in which he functioned was invariably at the absolute altitude of his choosing. When he embraced the cryptic vocabulary of Coptic Gnosticism, he lost his few remaining friends because it was impossible to follow the direction of his thoughts, and that was exactly what he wanted.

In Cairo Father played chess blindfolded and invariably he won. The positions of the pieces on the board were sharper in his mind's eye than the furniture of his own living room (where he was constantly scraping his shins and knocking over chairs).

But I keep digressing. What I wish to write about is a brief period of time in Egypt, one year, and above all, one summer that seems to stretch to infinity, a time of disquiet and loneliness. That year, and that summer, were a paradox—both intensely felt and numbing. The world passed before my eyes like an animated stage—distant, colorful, unattainable—and I, in my own chair, looked on, watchful and amazed, frightened, enchanted, and disembodied, too.

In Egypt, Father had taken to wearing a fez to wander as unobtrusively as possible. He looked Egyptian—we both did—so that Cairo embraced us unquestioningly, my father's limited but convincing Arabic sufficing during brief encounters with beggars and merchants and dragomen; and he spoke French.

One winter's day on an excursion to the Mouski, we passed the window of an ivory carver's shop that contained any number of charming miniatures: gazelles, tigers, monkeys, elephants, and the like. As he gazed at the animals—and I supposed he might elect to buy me one—Father began to cough and hum in a familiar way that meant he was about to make a brilliant move, or was excited by an idea. At that instant a small boy invited us into the shop, and offered us two little chairs on which to sit. The carver appeared then, beaming, and sent the boy off to fetch coffee. The tray set before us, the mystery of Father's excitement was revealed: If Father provided the drawings, could the carver make for him a chess set in which the goddesses and gods of the Egyptians and the Romans met face-to-face? Isis and Osiris, Horus and Amon Ra battling Juno and Jupiter and Neptune and Mars? Might sacred bulls confront elephants? He imagined the Egyptian pawns as ibises and the Roman pawns as archers.

This conversation took place in a boil of English, Arabic, and French; already the coffee tray was cluttered with sketches and ivory elephants—examples of sizes and styles. As the ivory carver and my father discussed the set's price and the time necessary for its completion, I sipped sherbet and explored the shadows. I found a stack of tusks as tall as myself and two pails: one contained ivory bracelets soaking to scarlet in henna and the other ivory animals soaking to the color of wild honey in black tea. As I looked the boy came over and with a flat stick stirred the carvings gently, all the while gazing at me with curiosity.

The shop was very old and smelled unlike any place I had ever been; I suppose it was the ivory dust on the air— all that old bone—the henna, the coffee, and the tea. It was a wonderful smell and soothing, so that for several instants I closed my eyes and slept.

When I awoke, the boy had vanished, leaving ajar a little door that opened onto the back alley. The alley led to a quarter entirely devoted to leather slippers stained green, and farther down an antiques seller's where I had seen a figure of hawk-headed Horus, the god of the rising sun, made of Egyptian paste and the size of a thumb. It had come from a tomb near Luxor.

The little figure had spoken to me with such urgency that, for the first time in my life, I had dared ask my father that he buy it. He did not take my request seriously. How could a thirteen-year-old possibly fathom the value of such a thing? Not that it was impossibly expensive—for in those days such pieces were still to be found easily enough on the market. But it was three thousand years old, and Father imagined a troubling eccentricity of character: my request seemed excessive. Had I inherited an immodest desire for luxury from my mother, who at that moment was having the hair removed from her armpits with hot caramel? (His own delight in luxury he did not question because compared to hers it was so tame: a collection of chess sets, a few articles of elegant clothing.)

Mother's extravagance and acute blondness were striking anywhere, but above all in Egypt. When in gold lamé she arrived late at a reception at the University Club, a hush descended upon the room. She preferred officers and had befriended a number of the Egyptian brass (including the young Nasser)—handsome men flourishing thick mustaches.

———

I was learning Arabic. To my delight I discovered if I said *egg'ga* I got an omelet, and *salata*, a salad. Father owned a charming little pocket dictionary with words in French, English, and Arabic, and incongruous illustrations of disparate objects. One page showed a Victorian piano, a British bobby, a sarcophagus, two sorts of cannon, a hula dancer, a radio singer, a caged tiger, a man singing in blackface, an airplane, a hand holding a pen, a pearl necklace, a salted ham, a taxicab, a star, a cobra, and a hat.

Each week my father and I returned to the ivory carver's shop, where the finished pieces accumulated. The Roman castles were Pompeian elephants decked out exactly as in an old print Father had hunted down in the university library; the print was based on a bas-relief uncovered in Pompeii. The little elephants had tusks that ended in spheres the size of small peas. These might be gilded and if they were: Should Isis wear a gold necklace and Amon

Ra a gold sun? *No.* Father was after simplicity. The Egyptians should be soaked in tea to darken them and this was all.

As he spoke my father fingered an Osiris four inches tall and completed that morning. He had the lithe body of a young, athletic man and the noble head of a falcon. In the guise of a crown he wore the solar disc encircled by a serpent, and in his hand he carried the Key of Life. Father said to me: "When Osiris was torn to pieces and his body tossed to the four winds, Isis, his beloved, searched the world until she found every part but the phallus, because it had been swallowed by a fish. She made him another—of precious wood or alabaster, no one knows. Then she laid his broken body on a perfumed bed and embraced him until he was whole again. And here he is!"

Smiling, Father raised the little figure to the sun that in its passage across the sky had suddenly filled the shop with light. Then, under his breath, he said with a bitterness so unique, so unexpected, that I was profoundly startled: *A thing that would not have occurred to your mother.*

———

Alone on my balcony in the afternoon, I would gaze out over the courtyard below, where Bedouins often camped. I could smell baking bread and hear the children singing. I loved to see the women suckle their little ones, and when the girls danced fearlessly I danced too, for in that quiet air the sound of their flutes and drums readily reached me.

They came because of the public water fountain and an ancient sycamore tree that kept the courtyard shady and cool. At its roots the Bedouins had nested their *goallah* or water pots, and I thought the word wonderful because it contained their word for God. I found a picture of a *goall* in the *Dracoman,* in a series including the sugarloaf-shaped hat of a dervish and a head of lettuce.

I would also gaze at the beautiful balconies across the courtyard, all pierced with patterns of stars. Sometimes a wood panel slid back and the small face of a child might appear, or that of a woman unveiled, her face impossibly pale, her eyes like the eyes of a caged animal, her throat and wrists circled in silver.

I had left all my toys behind but for a small box of glass and porcelain animals, and a green cloth I pretended was a vast meadow. But I was swiftly outgrowing these things. They paled beside the demands of my own slight body, awakening—I did not know to what, except that when each night I found pleasure beneath my small fingers, pleasure detonating like some sudden star, I imagined a blue man beside me, a blue man with the beautiful face of a bird of prey.

———

Today when we arrive to see the finished Osiris, the ivory carver is full of news. Just this morning in Alley of Old Time, a dervish sliced his belly open and revealed his entrails. A large number of people had gathered beside the carver's shop to throw coins at the dervish's feet and cry: *Allah is great! Praise Allah!* But even more extraordinary, the dervish had spontaneously taken his guts in both his hands and lifted them as though for the carver's inspection, before asking for a needle and thread to sew himself up again. After, he had limped away to die or to recover—"God," the carver says, "alone knows." The blood—and there was very little of it—was not washed away because the spot was considered by some to be holy ground. The ivory carver is eager to show us the blood, but Father at his most imperious says: *"L'extase ne m'interesse point."*

The next hour is characterized by silence, Father examining the new piece with extreme attention, the carver bent over his work—Jupiter—with exemplary intensity. Later on, as we are making our way back to Sharia el-Geish to hail a cab, we turn off too soon and, wandering in an unfamiliar maze of streets, find ourselves among the butchers' stalls, where Father bumps into a table piled high with several dozen skinned heads of sheep, shining with oil and ready for roasting.

Suddenly I see my father's fez rolling along the street and then Father bent in two and vomiting, spattering the knees of his white linen suit with filth. He vomits violently, in spasms, as little boys looking solemn gather in droves and one stunning man in a white turban offers my father a handkerchief moistened with orange-blossom water. Panting, Father grabs this to mop his face, and I see a wild look in his eyes, the look of the woman at the window of stars. Then, somehow, we are in a taxi speeding home, the generous man whom we will never see again diminishing like a genie behind us.

Throughout the ride Father's face remains plunged in the scented handkerchief. When we arrive at our building's gate, Father raises his eyes and I see that he is still terrified. He needs help counting change. For a moment he opens his mouth as if to apologize but says nothing, as though speaking demands too great an effort. To this day I cannot smell orange-blossom water without thinking of a cobbled street, a spoiled fez, my father's stained knees.

———

Father was ill for two months. A fever pinned him down so that he could barely move. When he was delirious, he raved that the head of gravity lay upon his heart and that it was made of oiled lead. He imagined that the Colossi of Memni had fallen onto his bed and were crushing him, that his own temple was filling with sand. In the fall we had seen stray dogs worrying the corpse of a camel. Father believed he was that camel.

He said he was being pulverized by Time—he spoke as if Time and Gravity were divine beings who despised him because he was merely mortal and made of frangible clay; those were his words: *frangible clay*. Finally—and this happened in May—his fever broke, his mind cleared, his mood lightened. Father began to mend. Within days we were able to walk to his chamber's balcony, which overlooked the street, to stand together cracking melon seeds between our teeth and tossing sweets to the organ grinder's monkey, who, when the music was over, pulled a tin plate from his pants, and a fork.

The following week Father was back to his desk catching up with his class work and his correspondence—he was at war with a dozen chess players in other countries. I was "Keeper of the Inkpot." Father teased: Should I spill any, or fail to fill his precious Mont Blanc correctly, I would be shipped off directly to the crocodile-mummy pits of Gebel Aboofayda! (The crocodile-mummy pits were illustrated on page 38 of the *Dracoman,* along with a fountain pen and a straitjacket.)

Now that Father was on his way to total recovery, we returned to Alley of Old Time to collect the completed chess set. It was splendid. Each Roman archer had distinct features, with bow lowered or raised, minute quivers (and these would soon be broken) in place. The stances of the ibises were variable and capricious: one was nesting and another about to take flight. Yet another, poised on one leg, was fishing, and one held a fish in its beak. Isis was very lovely—lovelier than Juno, who had a stern expression and a large hooked nose. Isis had two diminutive breasts; her soft belly was visible beneath the folds of her gown.

After we had admired the set at length and been served coffee—and I was given a special treat, a square of pink *loukoum* studded with pistachios and rolled in powdered sugar—the set was placed in its box, wrapped in brown paper, and tied with string. Then, as we departed, the ivory carver displayed a prodigious tenderness for my father by suddenly kissing his sleeve. We stepped out onto the street. It had been freshly watered and beneath the tattered awnings we walked in coolness.

"Before returning home," Father said, "let us pay a visit to the little Horus you once so admired. I imagine it is still vegetating in Hassan Syut's shop." This was such an unexpected delight that for an instant I stopped walking and leaned against my father's side, my arm about his waist.

The Horus was no longer there. It had, in fact, been sold some weeks earlier. However, Hassan Syut had something very unusual to show my father, and he went to the back of the shop where he sorted through a multitude of pale green boxes. He returned to the counter with an object wrapped in white linen, and with a flourish revealed a blackened piece of mummy. It was a hand cut off at the wrist, a child's hand carbonized by a three-thousand-years' soak in aromatic gum. It was a horrible thing, and my father let out a little cry of displeasure, perhaps despair: *Que c'est sale!*

For a reason unfathomable—for still I do not know my father's intimate history—Father was convinced the hand had been offered with malicious intention. "And you still a child," he said. *"Si fragile!"* We were making our way past row after row of green slippers. "Everywhere evil!" I thought I heard him say. *"Partout . . . le mal!"*

14

His voice was altered; he had begun to bleat as on occasion when he lost patience with my mother, and I, in the still of the night, would hear her return from the mystery that kept her so often away. On such nights it seemed to me that Mother's orbit was like that of a comet. Light-years away, when she approached us it was always on a collision course.

Father's words came quickly now; they spilled from his mouth with such urgency I could barely follow: "Evil is a *lack,* you see," I thought I heard him say. "A lack, a void in which darkness rushes in, a void caused by . . . by thoughtlessness, by narcissism, by insatiable desire. Yes, desire breeds disaster. *De toute façon,*" he said now, suddenly embarrassed, "those old bodies should be allowed to rest." I looked into his face. It seemed the hand had designated the darkest recess of his heart and had torn the delicate fabric of his eyes, for his eyes waxed peculiar, distant and opaque: minerals from the moon. I wondered: If a word was enough to create the world, could one artifact from Hell destroy it? The hand, reduced by time to a dangerous, an irresistible density, seemed, in the thinning air, to hover over us.

Father pulled a handkerchief from his vest pocket and pawed at his face. I believe I heard him mutter: "There is no rest." What did he mean? He hailed a cab, and I was aware that I dreaded going home.

The cab smelled of urine, and the windows—covered with a film of dust and oil—could not be rolled down, so that we traveled in a species of fog. When we arrived, I helped Father from the cab and held the gate open. When was it, I wondered, that he had become an old man?

The elevator was paneled with mirrors and the embrace of infinity vertiginous. I shut my eyes. Stepping into the hall, we heard music, and then, behind the door, Mother's thick voice, her voice of rum and honey, came to us; she was singing: *I made wine . . .*

Father did not ring but instead, holding the ivory chess set against his heart with one arm, fumbled for his keys.

From the lilac tree . . .

He was breathing with difficulty. I feared he was about to die. But the door was open now, and in a room flooded with the full sun of the late afternoon, Mother, her wet hair rolled up in a towel, was dancing, her naked body pressed to the body of a stranger. Seeing us, she held him to her tightly, and, her face against his chest, began to laugh—a terrible laughter that both extinguished the day and annihilated my father and me, severing us from her and from ourselves.

When my father took my hand, the chess set fell to the floor, seemingly in silence so loudly was the blood pounding in my ears. Father held my hand so tightly that it ached, an ache that was the ache of my heart's pain, exactly.

TWO

The Battlefields of Shiraz

It was my thirteenth summer. Father and I entered into a symbolic relationship with Mother of such intensity that even now I find it almost impossible to undo the mental knots we tied in our attempt to restrain her. That summer the city of Cairo took on the mystical and metaphysical features of one of those cryptic Roman paintings so prized by scholars in which each element has an allegorical significance: we saw signs of her everywhere. And I, who had finally managed not to think about her too much, I thought about her all the time. Her naked body rocking with laughter was the glyph beneath which the city pulsed; it haunted our nights—Father's and mine. When I visited the museum with Father—and, like the war games he played with Ramses Ragab, these visits took place in the early morning—I expected to see her materialize in every room. This was foolish; as much as she loved the Sporting

Club, Mother hated museums. But I wanted to see her; I wanted her to return. I chose to petition an admirable lion's head in Room 46. I wanted Mother back not because I loved her (I think, in fact, that I had come to violently dislike her), but because it was unbearable to know she was unleashed, like a force of nature.

I wanted to keep my eye on her, to watch her eat in that absent way she had, to hear her voice rising and falling in the night, to stumble upon her barefoot, her mind elsewhere, pacing the hallway before dawn. I also left instructions with a lion-headed waterspout. Understand that I had chosen lions only because of the fabulous head in Room 46—its beauty and size. Once that decision had been made, I found myself appealing to lions whenever I saw one. (Like Venice, Cairo was riddled with lions.)

After our visit to the museum, Father and I would find a garden and a quiet place to sit. We sat, often in silence, and sometimes for hours. Or we would take a long walk, to the Suq el-Nahassin, perhaps, to wander in the stunning cacophony, the sound of hammers making it impossible to think, the brass and copper trays and barber's basins, dazzling in the light of late morning, making it impossible to see.

"Egyptians," Ramses Ragab once said to me over breakfast (it was a habit of ours to share a late breakfast when he and Father had finished their game of war), "have always believed in magic." This all-pervasive way of seeing and being in the world had taken hold of Father and me.

"When I was a boy," Ramses Ragab said also, "my grandfather once sent me to Khedr el-Attar to buy a powder made of salamanders—a cure, or so he thought, for impotency."

Father and I would explore Khedr el-Attar, too, reeling under the influence of things we could not name but which filled the air with the scent of vanished times. Farther the streets smelled of new soap and then, suddenly, of lamb kidney toasting over open fires, reminding us that we had been wandering all day. Stumbling out of the maze of streets, Father would hail a cab and off we'd go to the Komais Restaurant, or the Paris Café. There, while waiting for dinner, we would gorge on pickles, Father mopping his face with his handkerchief and more than once muttering: "She's been here." Then, I too could smell Mother's perfume. When, after dinner, he overturned his empty cup and asked our waiter to read his fortune, the waiter said: "Your heart is empty," proving himself a worthy reader, "and it won't be filled for a long time."

I do not think Father was aware of how irrational he had become. He would look to the street and the sky for signs, signs that were the indication of Mother's movements, revelations as to the tenor of her moods and the nature of her thoughts. For the most part, Father, if clearly eccentric, appeared to be as rational as ever, but then something would occur, evidence of the—I can find only one word—*superstitious* nature of his thinking. For example, one morning as we loitered in a park, we saw a battle between two turtledoves. The female, coy as a cat, stood by.

Father said: "Your mother is like her. She will not wander far." And it is true, she was in the vicinity. She had taken rooms in the somewhat worn but elegant Hotel-Pension Viennoise, on Sharia Antikhana, not far from the museum.

I did not see it then as clearly as I do now; after all, I too was infected. But the empirical capacity of Father's mind—which had so often in the past impressed the world—had been violently disrupted. This new version of Father was more and more often incompatible with the old. However, it was summer and he was able to blame his odd behavior on the heat. Because, to a certain extent, he was aware of it. Just after the incident with the doves—we were crossing Soliman Pacha Place—he clicked his tongue as if to scold himself and said: "What nonsense I am speaking!" Caressing my cheek and grinning in that winning way he had, he added: "How exhausting summer is!" Yet, despite such moments of lucidity, Father persisted in what I can only call this new peculiarity of thought—peculiarity that at the time was part and parcel of the mysterious world around us: Cairo, its fabulous museums, the fantastical sprawl of Egypt, the desert so near at hand, Mother's maddening absence, and soon: Ramses Ragab's *Kosmètèrion*! That summer there was no such thing as *ordinary thinking*. The Universe had gone topsy-turvy, and the profusion of games—for they took place several times a week—was just a small part of it. We did not know it yet, but Mother was taking on the attributes of myth. It should come as no surprise that I once awakened from shattering dreams, my heart pounding, to find Father in the kitchen nibbling toast. We had both dreamed the same dream: that we had been bandaged up like corpses! (And surely this explains— why has it not occurred to me before?—my life's delight in liberating mummies from their gum-infested cloth to see the caramelized flesh clinging to the redundant, yet invariably startling, bone!)

———

Father, in his fez and holding a diminutive aerostatic globe, was stretched out on the Shiraz. As I entered the room, Ramses Ragab, dressed in a dazzling white linen suit and smelling of labdanum, stood and held out his hand. An astonishing hand: the nails were polished and shone like mirrors, and he was missing a thumb.

"We are," he explained with a self-mocking smile, "about to begin the battle of Fleurus."

They played at dawn because of the heat of summer. Father said he could think at dawn and at dusk only; the rest of the day he was "stunned." But I knew he played at war at dawn because his nights were cruel and long. The games gave him a reason to face the day; thanks to Ramses Ragab and the battle of Fleurus, he could look forward to the early hours rather than lie awake dreading another day without Mother.

As Father was engaged in the deployment of his troops, I asked Ramses Ragab—always a more precipitous player—

what the aerostatic globe, now hanging from the ceiling by a hook, was for.

"It is for Captain Coutelle," he explained, nervously smoothing his hair with those marvelous fingers; "armed with a telescope and suspended far above the capacity of the Austrian musketry, he shall watch the battle unscathed." Peering into the montgolfier's basket, I saw a little lead soldier. "Captain Coutelle is furnished with a large ball of twine," Ramses Ragab continued. "This he will use to send messages—wrapped around rocks—to the French army."

"If he sends too many messages," Father mumbled from the floor with apparent seriousness, "he'll lose his ballast and sail into the sun."

I learned that Captain Coutelle could not maneuver his balloon himself, but was pulled about by means of a heavy cord. This operation was manned by no less than one hundred and fifty foot soldiers. Rising to his knees, Father said wistfully: "This is how it all looked to Coutelle." Ruled by a set of handsome Bakelite dice, there was a chance the soldiers would all be wiped out by cannon fire and Coutelle lost to the wind. "He may land up on the North Pole," Father laughed, bitterly, I thought.

You have understood that in Father's house, chess was just the tip of the iceberg. The games he played with Ramses Ragab (and on occasion with Boris Popov, a Russian colleague at the university) were a direct expression of the profound shift that had taken place in his mind. "The player," Father liked to say, "as does any man, struggles against the imposition of rules. The rules are essential, but it is equally important to know how to bend them."

The playing field—in this case the sumptuous Shiraz, a carpet that looked like it had been woven of butterflies, and the very same Shiraz upon which Mother had entertained strangers—afforded a place where old patterns could be disrupted, new patterns found. For example, when Father and his friend played at Waterloo, Napoleon always had a chance, as did the dervishes at Dongola. (Later that summer Kitchener's head would be set out on a toothpick pike.) Ruled by what he himself called *gamblesomeness,* Father, when he was not playing chess, played at war—and he played (the words belong to Ramses Ragab) *a deep game.* He never played poker—"a low game and a game of cheats"—nor Go (because he invariably lost). I should add that Father sometimes used the word *game* in a novel way. He had a "game" of Austrians, a "game" of Abyssinians, and even a "game" of camels. If Father was ruled by gamblesomeness, I think of this now, Mother *was* game. Her playing field was love, if not the love of Father. Nor, it is clear now, did she love me.

To continue: As beautiful as these games were, as beautiful as Father's lead soldiers looked that morning set out on the blazing hearth of the Shiraz, their beauty was not the point. When he played at war, Father left the twentieth century behind and so was able to circumvent its indignities. Father was not after an aesthetic charge so much as fulfilling a magical aim. Time and time again, all summer long, Father and Ramses Ragab would alter the course of history. This is not to say that aesthetics were absent. My father painted his armies with the delight of a pastry cook icing cakes. He relished sticking feathers to helmets with a spot of glue, and he had set out a naked brunette—to scale—standing up to her knees in a little painted pool; "The victor," he grinned, "may claim her."

"Beauty is double sixes," Ramses Ragab had laughed. "She is ascendant."

"I do not blame her," Father said then, and it was—I am certain—the first time he had referred in public to what had transpired. He said nothing else. Ramses Ragab dropped to his knees and looked on—we both did—as Father continued to set out his men, row after row of them.

Beauty is ascendant. I thought the remark obscure, but then I found it compelling. I had, just the week before, spent another dimly mysterious and tender morning along with Father at the Cairo museum, looking at the figures and forms of the dead. The alabaster faces of Queen 'Ahmòse-Nefertiri and Princess Sit-Hathor-Iunet, and even General Sepi—although his coffin is the oldest in the museum—were so beautiful they took the breath away. (General Sepi's corneas are carved of rock crystal!)

"Let the battle begin!" Father then exclaimed, easing himself back on the heels of his fancy leather pumps. The room took on the scent of mastic; in the kitchen our servant Beybars was busy fumigating the coffee cups. In a moment he would bring the coffee to the two men on a tiny tinned copper tray—a charming ritual that was taking place all over the city.

"On commence!" Ramses Ragab agreed as with a certain violence he rattled the dice in his fist. The men tossed to see who would go first. *"En avant!"* cried Father.

I left then, and wandered into Mother's abandoned room. Her dressing table, now distressingly free of clutter, had been a place of passion. At that table, before her mirror—a thing of such splendor and so heavy it would take two strong men to carry it off when, a week or so later, she sent for it—she had made her mortal face into something (Ramses Ragab's word comes to me) *ascendant.*

His word was also hers. Mother owned a book—one of the few books I had ever seen her read—that offered a studio photograph of Irene Dunne wearing pearls and standing beside a horrible faux Chinese lamp, in what Mother called an *ascendant* pose. But if you could tear your eyes from her ideal qualities, you would see that the carpet above which Ms. Dunne, in very high heels, appeared to levitate—was both threadbare and missing an entire corner. Clearly the photo was meant to be cropped. *Odd* (Mother's word for me even then), it was the missing corner that captured my attention. It was a reminder of mortality, of things gone missing.

"She's just like one of those twenty-first dynasty corpses!" I exclaimed when, in an attempt to educate me, Mother released the precious volume from her vanity drawer.

"What the *fuck*?" growled Mother. Turning the page, she examined a photograph of Virginia Mayo about to sit down in a chair.

"Like the corpse of Ramses II," I insisted. "With pepper up the nose. I mean . . ." I blurted, stubborn despite the withering influence of my mother's outrage, "she only, uh . . . *looks* ascendant." I began to tell her of the extraordinary things I had learned during those precious moments when Ramses Ragab and Father would leave the battleground for breakfast—when she was at the baths or who knows where—and engage in what Father called "Ragab's Mysteries." I told Mother that the Pharaoh's brain had been pulled from the skull through the nostrils with an iron hook, and his anus plugged with an onion.

"Not an *ordinary* onion—"

"Don't be a jerk." Mother inhaled her cigarette deeply.

"Tut's nails were tied on with strings," I continued somewhat didactically (a trait inherited from Father), "so that they wouldn't fall out." I felt like sobbing. And did not explain, that if I was smitten by corpses, corpses—it must be said—that had been thoroughly washed inside and out with spiced wine, and whose body cavities were packed with cassia and myrrh—I also looked with profound interest at the erections of Pharaohs—always so unabashedly ubiquitous on the painted walls of tombs, and the vases and chests and scrolls that were stacked throughout the museum in an irresistible state of disarray. (I suppose this means my adolescence was passed under the sign of *strangeness*—although this occurs to me only now.)

Mother sighed, shrugged, and studied the rules for getting in a chair:

Don't slick your skirts down over your buttocks. I never see a woman slicking her skirts over her buttocks and reaching out with her rear without thinking, "Well, here it is—where shall I put it?"

THREE

The Kosmètèrion

"Cassia, myrrh, lavender, orris, santal, rose, bergamot, anise, almond . . . even as a child I loved these things," Ramses Ragab once told me, "for their fragrances which caused me no end of delight, and for the mysteries of their medicinal properties which evoked the deepest reveries I had ever known and the greatest bliss. And I wondered: If a corpse could be secured from the immodest ravages of time by the precious oils of plants, then a savant use of them must protect the beauty of the living—not an original thought, but compelling to me. I decided to devote myself to chemistry—analytical, biological, and pathological, and pharmacology—chemical and galenical; I studied toxicology and crystallography; I even studied alchemy! Then one marvelous afternoon I came upon Publius Ovidus Naso's *Cosmetica . . .*"

And so we come to that extraordinary place of his

invention, Ramses Ragab's marvelous *Maison des Parures,* his *Kosmètèrion.*

———

The day we visited the *Kosmètèrion* for the first time, the trees of Cairo were filled with the sudden hum of cicadas. It was a hot, limpid day and we walked without haste, having set out early. When we reached the El Ezbekièh gardens, a vendor sold us tea boiled in and poured from the same pot. We sat in the shade of an ancient cedar tree and very slowly sipped our tea.

Even after all these years, the *Kosmètèrion* continues to have a compelling hold on my imagination. That summer Father joked: "All roads lead to the *Kosmètèrion!*" After a moment's hesitation he added, "When they do not lead to your mother." *Centrifugal* is a word that comes to mind.

The *Kosmètèrion* was situated in the soûk el-Attarin and, as it turned out, very near the rue el Halouagi—a favorite haunt of ours because of its many booksellers, including a shop that specialized in militaria, and where Father had found a rare copy of Batterhill's *Ashurbanapal* and I *The Arabian Nights*—so provocatively illustrated I did not show it to Father, who supposed I had pocketed a child's version. Even the bookseller was unaware, taking my *piastres* without comment. What I had glimpsed were two pages protected by tissue paper and painted with cheerful simplicity: *The Operations of Nature* and *The*

Divine Pleasures of Marriage. On these pages rosy men and women in dizzying configurations were arranged like pieces of fruit.

But now there was no time to be tempted by books. Without further delay we made our way down a narrow impasse in the deep shade of a half-dozen ancient Persian houses to the *Kosmètèrion*'s indigo door. When Father pulled a leather strap to ring the bell, the door swung open with a groan and we were in a vestibule tiled blue from floor to ceiling, filled with fresh bouquets of flowers and silent but for the ticking of an old Italian clock. A serious boy who smelled of limes led us to a room where a thousand bottles of glass burned on mirrored shelves. There a smaller boy with moles on his face sat on the tiled floor nibbling seeds. The moles studded his cheeks and the crests of his eyebrows and were so attractive I was not surprised when Ramses Ragab told us he had named a bubble bath *Zaki's Moles.*

"Zaki," Ramses Ragab explained, embracing Father and me, "is my *second nose.* Quit dreaming away the hours, Zaki! *Au travail!*" Ramses Ragab's *second nose* leapt to his feet and spun across the room, snapping up bottles from shelves and jars from under counters: bottles of glass, of alabaster and calcite; jars of porcelain—some white, some glazed black; jars of deep blue glass.

"I have in this vessel," Ramses Ragab said with mock gravity as he lifted a green jar and held it up for us to see, "a Javanese clay said to explain the beauty of the women of that country, who nibble on it. And here—" he pointed to a shelf—"cakes of true grey amber!" He broke one in two and showed us how it was flecked inside with white. "Grey amber never smells of fish," he told us, "but only of flowers." Meanwhile Zaki continued to dervish about the room, spiriting little boxes of powder seemingly from the air.

"Is it the full moon, Zaki," Ramses Ragab wondered, "that has you spinning like a top?" In answer, Zaki began to juggle atomizers. "Come! Stop your antics and put those here, *carefully* on the counter." Ramses Ragab began opening drawers. "Essences," he told us. "Aloes wood, tamarind, exotic gums and *even soap!*" With a flourish, Zaki set one on the counter. Bristling with pieces of ginger and pepper, it was as big and yellow as an orange.

"Un petit savon stimulant!" Zaki pretended to scrub himself all over. *"C'est Farouk—"*

"Farouk once sent his barber to buy twelve dozen," Ramses Ragab said, "but the king never paid for anything and so I turned him away." Trembling with mock rage, Zaki pointed to the door. As Ramses Ragab told his story, Zaki stood like a statue, glowering and pointing at the door.

"Turned out the king!" he shouted suddenly and to my delight did a neat somersault that ended at my feet.

"No," said Ramses Ragab laughing. "Not the king. The barber. If only he'd drowned in his bath! Well, Egypt's rid of him at last."

"The barber or the king?" I asked. My understanding of Egyptian politics was woefully limited.

"The king." Ramses Ragab smiled at me indulgently. "The barber is still around, in the Khan el Kalili baking cakes."

"*Très bons!*" Zaki rubbed his belly and rolled his eyes.

"Zaki," Ramses Ragab scolded. "You know you must not buy cakes from the barber. Remember how he threatened to shave me with a saw? How he set the butcher's beard on fire with a Bunsen burner? How he broke Abu Nissir's leg? Come now, Zaki! I've told you not to buy cakes from the barber!"

"*Plus jamais,*" Zaki promised. Thoughtfully he stroked the soap.

"You know about Farouk, of course," Ramses Ragab said. "His affection for the contents of other people's closets? Their motor cars? His sidekick who fleeced dinner guests of their lighters, loose change, cuff links, and car keys? Who carried a pair of tiny scissors to cut the brass buttons off blazers?"

"We knew of Farouk's prodigious size," said Father.

"Farouk was so fat," said Ramses Ragab, "that had he stepped on Samoa it would have sunk." He pulled a stopper, held my wrist, and left a fragrant, dark green drop on my skin. Shyly, the *second nose* approached and whispered: "*Cyprinium!*"

"Made," Ramses Ragab explained, "with the henna of Fayum. Around the time I decided to do this work," he continued, unstopping another bottle and spelling the air with a fragrance like raw honey, "I had an unforgettable dream. I was swimming in a tropical sea above a reef of coral that seemed to go on forever. I knew that each single animal was a fragrance waiting to be invented. Then, before my eyes, the coral was transformed into an infinity of wild roses."

"What a marvelous dream!" Father smiled at his friend with affection.

"I should add that before I fell asleep, I had been reading a magical papyrus of late antiquity. It described how the spirit or vital breath of things is seduced, seized, and locked away . . ." He pearled my wrist with nard.

"You are a magician," said Father. "A performer of pneumatic magic! And"—he glanced at Zaki, who at that instant was standing on his hands—"you surround yourself with djinn!"

As if to demonstrate that this was so, Zaki leapt up and an instant later had put a huge jar on the marble counter. It was a face cream lifted from Ovid, made of honey, barley, and eggs.

"Zaki is very precious to me," Ramses Ragab said as his assistant nibbled seeds. I noticed then that Zaki's left ear was missing its lobe. "He was a street urchin once," Ramses Ragab would tell us later over tea. "One day he stole a piece of fruit and its price was exacted with the fruit seller's knife. Ah, Zaki! My own hashshásheen! Greed will undo you. And I"—he held up his maimed hand—"lost a finger in the fray!"

———

Many, but by no means all, of the perfumes Ramses Ragab manufactured were known to the ancients and then forgotten.

"It is my desire," Ramses Ragab said, "to bring each and every one back to life. The true *kyphi* of Edfu, mendesium, amarakinon . . ." He told us that once he had risked his life swimming in a snake-infested lagoon because the yellow lilies growing in the slime had a fragrance that was the point of confluence he searched for. The lilies were too few to harvest, and they grew nowhere else. It was impossible to transplant them, and in the attempt he had destroyed what was there. He said: "I shall never forgive myself this act of savagery." But the scent of the lilies in the afternoon air, the quality of the day's light, and even the odor of the lagoon all conspired to haunt him. "I had come upon the scent of the precise point where heaven meets earth," he said. "The scent of Eden. And behind it: the mysterious scent of transgression." How did he describe the scent of transgression?

"Metal. *Brass,* more precisely. Bruised green cardamom. Rushes . . . Transgression smells *green,*" he said, decisively.

Father appeared to be dreaming on his feet.

"I am thinking that a bottle of perfume is like a Pharaoh's tomb," he said. "It contains a body awaiting resurrection!" Pleased with himself, Father gazed humming at the mirrored shelves as Ramses Ragab gave me a crumb of pisang that, with my finger, I dissolved in a drop of oil. Suddenly a profoundly sexual scent filled the air.

"When Tutankhamun's tomb was opened," Ramses Ragab said, "small calcite bottles were found still holding preparations that, when melted by the skin's heat, smelled of spikenard."

"What does spikenard smell like?" I asked.

"Patchouly," he said. "Valerian."

"What do *I* smell like?" Clearly the magic of the place had emboldened me.

"Grapefruit," he answered without hesitation. "Grapefruit, green sandalwood, and a new box of lead pencils. Come!"

Our host was on the move, and we happily followed him out into the shade of his garden down a path leading to a second blue door. Passing through a dim yet orderly chamber in which roots, thorny branches, and bark were stored, we saw quills of cassia and cinnamon tied in bundles, and jars of oil and the fat of geese that the ancients had used in their sacred preparations and kept safe in lovely vases of stone. From there a corridor brought us to the *Kosmètèrion*'s beating heart: a laboratory filled with the fragrance of roses, roses Ramses Ragab had planted in Fayum:

"The sufis say that when the roses exhale they whisper: *Allah! Allah!*"

Just as we entered the laboratory, a black-eyed girl, not much older than I, glanced our way fleetingly, with an expression so haughty I was stunned. She was pressing fresh rose petals to a large sheet of pure white tallow. Her hands fluttered like moths as she gently pressed the petals down and then, when the sheet of tallow was completely covered, took the petals up again to discard them. She would repeat this process until the tallow was saturated with fragrance. Near her a small boy was tearing more roses apart and dropping the petals into a large basket. A few wasps that had made their way in from the garden were busy drowning in a vinegar trap; the room was silent but for the wasps' death battles.

"This is Abu"—Ramses Ragab indicated the boy who was smiling at us shyly—"and this lovely creature is Sakkiet." Sakkiet tossed her head and gave me another haughty look. Yet, despite her evident dislike of me, I stood captivated by her hands, her swift fingers that seemed to dissolve in the air. I imagined that here time was not counted in seconds, but in the petals of roses. Each atom of air was scented with roses. I longed to be the girl, Sakkiet.

My reverie was disrupted by this odd phrase of Ramses Ragab's: ". . . The requisites of randomness—" which Father repeated questioningly—Father who feared randomness and yet courted it daily. Ramses Ragab had been talking about empiricism, the empirical sequences so essential to the manufacture of perfume: "The requirements of uniqueness," he said next. Then as I turned toward him, to see him clearly for the first time, he continued to speak with growing enthusiasm, his eyes taking on a deep amber glow, a liquid quality like the raw honey in jars of transparent glass lined up on a high shelf behind him—

". . . In fact," he was saying, "each element, because it is a thing of Nature, each blossom of henna, each grain of pepper—" and I was taken, not only by his eyes, but the planes of his face, his features, which I realized were very fine. And his mouth. His mouth was beautiful. "—each grain of pepper, so like the next it is impossible to tell one from the other, has properties of its own. If this difference is not readily perceptible, it is revealed upon close inspection. A harvest of roses will differ dramatically from one place to the next, one year to the next. I must see to it that despite divergences, the finished perfumes are as alike as possible, unchanged year after year, all the while keeping in mind that an unexpected or random note may be exactly what I am ideally, *ideally*," he repeated, "looking for. The subtle yet marvelous divergence that will make the fragrance more active than before, more complex, more seductive, *astonishing* somehow. So that the one who wears it will never be forgotten." He smiled at me when he said: *Never be forgotten.*

"Here lies the heart of the problem," he continued, "to be empirical yet attentive to the subtle shifts due to some unknown, unexpected sequence of events, for example an unusual conformation of the soil, that deviance or anomaly that will make the world spin a little faster." With his finger he placed a drop of perfume beneath my ear, there where the pulse was beating. He said: "The beauty of absolute certainty always embraces the subversion of absolute doubt." The scent was named Metopium. In that instant, as he breathed the word *Metopium,* the exoticism of Cairo gave way to the exotic mind of Ramses Ragab.

Father, who had said little, muttered with a now familiar, bitter irony: "The *stench* of absolute doubt!" When he saw that we both looked at him with concern, he snorted apologetically.

"*Ah! Mais . . .* I've not offered you a thing!" Putting his arm around Father's shoulders, Ramses Ragab hurried us to a small interior garden where we sipped black tea and devoured "cat's tongues" ("In the land of the sphinx one should eat nothing else," said Father), little round confections flavored with jasmine and neroli, and those inimitable pastries called "gazelle's horns"—an unintentional reminder of Father's cuckolding. With that maddening habit of his, Father, showing all his teeth, said: "I did not know that horns could be so sweet!" Although many years have passed, I can clearly see the gap in his teeth: "A syphilitic ancestor!" he liked to joke, which made him look simultaneously sinister and droll. (Although when he was happy, it only added to his charm.)

"Egyptians have always loved sweets as much as they have always loved perfume," said Ramses Ragab then, tactfully ignoring Father's remarks. "Even these sweetmeats are perfumed with blossoms." He launched a story of a slanderer who, dying of cancer of the tongue, was cured by a celestial tray of pastry perfumed with mastic.

———

That afternoon I heard the curious vocabulary of the perfumer for the first time. *Vulgar* was said with a sneer, *ven-*

omous shadow with reverence. A scent might be *milky* or *metallic, sulphurous* or *chalky.* One was to be worn with linen the color of sand or snow; one was *prodigious,* one had a *velvet body,* another's was *deep red,* or, if worn in stormy weather, *red veering to black;* one smelled of *old silver* and *cedar forests,* and yet another was *symphonic*—"unlike the stenches my rivals call perfume but which are no better than the urine of asses and camels!" The great perfumes of ancient Egypt: *hekenou, medjet, sefet,* and *nekhenem* he called: *irresistible.* Their names alone seemed to darken the garden air with a mysterious smoke.

When Ramses Ragab said *cassia,* it sounded like the hiss of a snake. When he described the ginger grown in Malabar, he made our mouths water. *"Nagrunga!"* he breathed. "This is the name for the bitter orange. It comes from India. If you listen you can hear the Spanish word *naranja,* the Italian *naranzi . . ."*

"Naranzi . . ." I repeated, my mouth full of sugar. *"Nagrunga . . ."* He told us that the scent Pliny loved best was called *nardinon;* he told us that in the traditions of Egypt the virtue of perfume was above all aphrodisiac, for example: to incite the sexual ardor of the groom. The bride, however, was expected to remain passive, although she sat in a cloud of scent on a scented bed.

"Else she be her husband's whore," Ramses Ragab explained. "Not his wife."

"Aha!" Father barked cryptically.

———

Later that day as we left the *Kosmètèrion,* a tall Cairene with very black eyebrows and vividly hennaed hair brushed past us with her nose in the air. She was voluptuous, dressed as Mother often was, in a white silk suit, a scarf of gold lamé tied at her neck.

"There she is," Father whispered in my ear in that dreadful new way he had, "sent by the archons to taunt me!" I must admit that I could not help but wonder if Mother was setting a style. Fantastically, as if he had read our minds, Ramses Ragab, who had left us briefly to greet the woman and accompany her to the mirrored room where Zaki took over, said:

"Human life gathers potent forms to itself. We call these forms 'coincidences.' But they are random only in the way spots on a leopard are random. In other words, they are powers, perhaps unknown divinities, and their appearance in our lives is a symptom of our sickness, or a revelation of our destiny. I like to think that if one is attentive to the world's wind and one's movement through it, then the path one needs to follow will be clearly visible. These 'forms,' " he continued, "are more than signs, you see; they are *inevitabilities* to be deciphered at all cost!" He pressed a little bottle of essence of rose—fixed with santal and thinned with oil—into my hand.

"My gift," he said, "for you, Elizabeth."

Just then the Cairene, in all her splendor, appeared scowling at the door with impatience.

"I did not come to spend the day with that *efreet* of

yours," she said, "Monsieur Ragab!" As she spoke she lifted her arms and caressed the back of her neck, causing her breasts to swing forward. Her gesture, the compelling shapeliness of her body, evoked Mother so convincingly she took my breath away. The gesture, like the gesture a magician makes with his wand, multiplying doves at will, seeded the city with women—voluptuous women smelling of henna and smoke, of the metal knife the moment it halves the apple, of brocade, of nostalgia, of transgression. I felt the press of women's bodies coming at us from all directions.

As Father and I retreated into the blazing sun, the rising dust and clamor of the street, the city of Cairo gave way to a forest of the mind. A forest where female animals offered themselves to love and in broad daylight were mounted before the eyes of the world.

FOUR

My Mother's Mirror

One morning Father and I walked to the museum with Popov, Father's Russian colleague. As we explored those prolific rooms, Popov told me that in Egypt's earliest graves, the bodies of the dead had not been mummified but only buried in sand. Sometimes the hot, dry sand had admirably preserved them. Later in the day we sat in the shade of the third pyramid. Father was happily preoccupied with the virtues and perils of a desert war. Inevitably a few soldiers would be lost to the sand: "Yet such a game would well be worth the risks. A virtuous, *virtuous* sport here in the shadow of Mykérinos!" Poking about with his salad fork, Popov found a desiccated finger and presented it to me. Although this ruined Father's mood, I eagerly accepted it: a perfectly preserved finger with a ring of serpentine adhering to the flesh.

"I will keep it forever!" I said with real enthusiasm.

"Iz sumzing!" (And Popov could never speak without foaming at the mouth, his spittle flying into our faces although we sat at a fair distance.) "This digit here, iz not juzt creepsi, da?" I burst out laughing. Father, too, could not resist Popov's "creepsi, da?" and the three of us roared with laughter, the fragment lying like a dead caterpillar in my lap. But then I recalled Ramses Ragab's lost thumb and for the rest of the day was silent, as silent as my brooding father so often was; I fear Popov had a dreary time of it. I was imagining the enraged fruit seller leaping into the street as he raised his knife to slice off Zaki's ear, Ramses Ragab passing at that moment, reaching for the fruit seller's arm, his blood and Zaki's raining into the street. When, the following evening, I asked Ramses Ragab what had happened next, I learned that he and Zaki had been arrested and that he had paid a heavy fine to keep Zaki from prison. "Cairo is a cruel city" is what he said. "But then what city is not cruel, sooner or later?" After a moment he added: "Zaki was well worth his price; for Zaki I would give my entire hand. He has an extraordinary capacity, you see. He can tell if a grain of musk comes from Kaboul or Pendjab; a spoon of honey from the hills of Greece or Dogonland. Together we will discover a fragrance that will bring us both immortality." He laughed at the outrageousness of this claim. Sensing my confusion, he explained: "I don't believe in immortality."

That night I dreamed a hazardous dream, exceptional for its sensuality. I dreamed I was standing in the laboratory of the *Kosmètèrion* along with Ramses Ragab, and that it was he who was pressing the fresh petals into the white tallow. His fingers moved swiftly, taking petals from the deep basket and pressing them down with tenderness. As he worked the surface of the tallow pearled with moisture. I awoke in a room scented with roses; my body, too, was scented.

It was after ten. Father and Ramses Ragab had been at war for over two hours. Beybars was nearly done preparing breakfast, and the sweet smell of onions frying in oil filled the air. In a few minutes we would all sit down together at a fantastic claw-footed table that I adored. A vestige of colonial times, it had come with the house.

When I saw Ramses Ragab, I melted; it was as though the dream had somehow given him to me. He kissed me on both cheeks in greeting and we stood alone together in the little alcove that led to the dining room waiting for Father who, humming to himself, was putting soldiers into boxes. Father had just lost the battle of Fleurus. Fastidiousness was his way of dealing with defeat. I broke the silence by exclaiming:

"I dreamed about the *Kosmètèrion*!" Ramses Ragab was delighted.

"I dream about it every night," he said. "Last night I dreamed a way to extract essences without any pressure whatsoever. I had invented a new sort of air that I kept in a very large glass vessel shaped like the human heart. There was an elegant web of glass tubing through which I dropped fistfuls of petals. They produced the most exquisite vapor! How significant it all seemed, and how simple! As soon as I awoke I attempted to draw the vessel and its web of glass; in fact, I have it with me . . ." He dug into his pocket and pulled out a piece of folded paper. The sketch was very strange. It looked—as best as I can remember—like this:

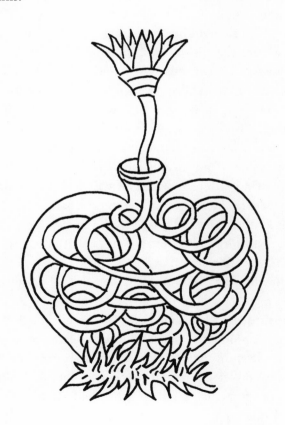

"You see?" he said, "how impossible it is?" He laughed and his marvelous eyes, so black they might have been rimmed with kohl, needled my heart. (I choose the word *needled* because this is precisely how it felt.)

"But . . . how thoughtless of me!" He tried to take the sketch back, but I held to it fast. "You will think your dream does not interest me; it *does*." I bit my lip and crossing my toes said only: "I dreamed about the petals in the tallow . . ." I thought he was teasing when he said:

"We had the same dream!"

Now, as I write this down, I think this was so: his dream's essence had filled my own nostrils as I slept.

"Everything may be read," Ramses Ragab said that morning as Father continued to tuck his soldiers into their boxes as if into bed—a familiar sight that only now strikes me as strange—"our dreams most of all." As I gazed at his little drawing with real interest he added: "I am certain that somewhere in the recesses of my mind a part of me is busy designing the impossible vessel. Who knows? Perhaps one day its feasibility will take me by surprise. But tell me, Elizabeth. Do you dream often?"

"Just like the Cairo-Palace Cinema!" Father called out. "Every night."

It is true that I dreamed every night, as though dreaming were a product of our family's disintegration, a way to fill the vacuum created by Mother's departure. These dreams were—it seems clear to me now—about awakening from the perpetual blindness that had characterized us both, Father and me. They illuminated not only the void she had left in her wake, but a void that, if it had never been acknowledged, had always been palpable; the void of her disinterested presence, an absence that even as a small child I chose to call: *Something gone missing.* That summer, *something gone missing* extended itself, embracing a number of things: not only a finger lost in sand, Ramses Ragab's imperfect hand, the missing lobe of Zaki's ear (and soon a number of lead soldiers); not only my mother—but all those who had once worn rings and perfume and had forever vanished. And the minutes themselves that passed, life's precious book of days and hours. Beauty's vanishment also. My mother's own battle with time. Her empty mirror.

In my first dream of the *Kosmètèrion,* Ramses Ragab filled all absences. The dream was about finding and keeping. Finding and keeping love and beauty, and also: keeping alive.

"You are still dreaming." Ramses Ragab's warm voice brought me back to the room, the late morning sun, the smells of the breakfast Beybars was setting out on the table. Ramses Ragab yawned and stretched, and I was stunned by the easy beauty of the moment.

"I should never have attacked you in the marsh!" Father joined us then. "A foolish, foolish move!" He held out his arms. "Good morning!"—he embraced me briefly— "dearest daughter. *En avant!*" Grinning, he led us in to breakfast, his fez at an odd angle.

We sat down together in a room dappled with light and gazed with appetite at the small feast. If Father's games were an exercise in containment, the playing field laid out like a garden, so Beybars' breakfasts: the salads, cheeses, eggs, beans, and pickles—O! The wonderful pickles Beybars made for us, singing plaintive love songs all the while!—plotted in elegant patterns, were a demonstration of Beybars' own version of harmony. Beybars' warrior's feasts infused the house with tangible joy and—I am sure of it—kept it from collapsing in on itself like a deck of cards.

"I should bottle the volatile particles of Beybars' breakfasts," Ramses Ragab said, slicing into a wheel of sheep's cheese so rich it tasted like cake.

"You'd need to bottle his songs, too!" I said. "And the smell of pigeons roosting on the kitchen balcony." I saw that he was gazing at my naked arm. It occurred to me that I should buy some bangles of colored glass (although Mother believed in what Father had in better times laughingly called the "Gold Standard"). How I hated gold! I would wear glass. The bangles would knock together like dice in a fist. They would catch the light of the sun. They would catch the eye.

"How could I have known I'd roll fours!" Father agonized. "Three times, *three times*! In succession!"

"The *marsh*," said Ramses Ragab. "Your army was lost before the battle began. They're all dead now!" He pretended to gloat. "Or wandering about crazed with fever. The rest are all prisoners of war." He pulled a soldier from his breast pocket and handed it to Father.

"Aha!" Father grinned, the gap between his front teeth making him look a little deranged. "Coutelle! I thought he was sailing the stratosphere!"

"How small he is!" I said.

"See to it that he doesn't sail into the omelet." Father made this request with apparent seriousness.

Outside a vendor called *"Khass! Khass!"* And Beybars came in to ask if we wanted fresh lettuce for supper. Before Father could reply, Ramses Ragab said:

"They won't be needing lettuce as I intend to invite them to dinner. We shall eat lamb with our fingers," he smiled at me, "in the light of a single sequin blinking in the navel of a belly dancer." A belly dancer, whose agitations would intrigue and embarrass me, simultaneously. Yet she would *keep her head quiet,* as Mother's book admonished:

> There is no allure, no feminine grace, in a bobbing, restless head.

After war, and fortunately for me, conversation drifted to the vivid talk I loved. Ramses Ragab and Father both enjoyed astonishing each other, or, at least, attempting to, with information about extraordinary events, phenomena, or people—such as Athanasias Kircher, that "metaphysical alchemist" who in the early seventeenth century attempted to create a system of thought that would embrace human experience in its entirety.

"He believed the Egyptian hieroglyphs were a mystical and all-inclusive vocabulary," Ramses Ragab said, causing Father to shift nervously in his chair—a habit of his when hearing about a thing for the first time. (It is curious that Father, who delighted in the acquisition of knowledge from books, was made nervous when another person revealed things unknown to him. He resented it as much as he would resent learning a new rule from an opponent in the middle of a game. He once confided to me that as the rules for the battles that took place on the Shiraz were all of his own invention, he could never be "brought up short." To tell the truth, I had come to hate games—and this at an early age—because Father was not above inventing new rules himself.)

"Kircher believed in the ideality of the hieroglyphs and the cosmical system they animated," Ramses Ragab continued. Lost in thought, he caressed his lips with his fingers. "People may laugh at Kircher today, but his attempt to grasp the hieroglyphs' meaning was noble and inspired." He might have punched a hole in the air, so breathless his intensity made me.

"What does it mean," I managed, "the *ideality* of the hieroglyphs?"

"Only that the world is mind; that our minds are capable of piercing its mystery; that—because they are inventions of mind—the hieroglyphs are also the embodiment of all that is divine."

"But why?"

"Because mind is divine."

"Kircher thought the hieroglyphs were a way of reading the Book of Nature," Father offered. "What's more: they *were* the Book of Nature!" Had he known about Kircher all along? Who could say?

"Kircher might have called it an 'ideal coherence,' " Ramses Ragab offered. "And in a way, Kircher was on the right track. The glyphs *are* potencies. After all, for those who know how to read them, they have the power to restore a lost world."

Despite Father's possible bluffing, the excitement this discussion generated was such I have never forgotten it. Looking back, it seems to me that like the finger Popov found in the sand, it, too, pointed out the direction my own mind would take. Now, after all these many years, when I enter a tomb and read the walls, I am thrust body and soul into vibrancy. The tomb is ascendant. It is more than the intermediary between earth and heaven: *it is the point of conjunction.*

In the painted tombs of Egypt, the enigma of separateness is resolved. The world and its seasons are without end. Here I am confronted with the paradox that has come to exemplify my life: all my senses awaken in these houses of the dead. Here the wheat is always green, the fennel sweet, the lilies blooming. The tomb is the place of perfect fragrancy.

And in the laboratory, when I lift off the mummy's gilded face and free the body from its linen, plucking up the precious amulets as they appear: the scarabs, the solar discs, the frogs and eyes, the sunken body—whittled down in the vortex of the fleeting years—takes on that "ideal coherence" of which Ramses Ragab spoke. When this happens, I see my own father sleeping there, or Ramses Ragab, perhaps. If the body is a woman's body, I see myself. I do not think: *This is how I will one day be.* I think: *She was once like me.* You see: each body is a Book of Nature also. You will not believe how much one discovers in the reading of a body! For example: I have often found amulets in the form of fingers: always two fingers together and always carved of a dark stone such as obsidian. They represent the fingers of the one who clears the mucus from the nostrils and the mouth so that the breath of life may enter the newborn's lungs. This amulet is often joined by another representing the knife used to cut the umbilical cord. Whenever I find it, I make a quick (superstitious!) gesture across my own belly. In this way I have, over and over, severed ties with Mother.

In classic Western art—Rembrandt's etchings, for example, his biblical scenes—areas are left unfinished, areas of light, perhaps the light of grace, against which the weighty shadows of time are heaving. If there are figures in these vacancies, they are wisps animated only to, in a breath, perish. But in Egypt's painted tombs, there are no empty spaces; there are no shadows. Even dead, people are muscled and vigorous; even the night is bright with starlight. There is no wind, whereas in Rembrandt the world never ceases to shudder in the grip of weather.

Back to Kircher for an instant. He was the first person to observe and comment upon the spots on the face of the sun. "The joke was that he'd gone mad," said Ramses Ragab, "staring at the sun."

———

Later, in the intense heat of the day, I bathed and scented myself with the rose perfume. While Father painted soldiers in his study, leaning over them like a kabbalist over his books, I undressed and stood before Mother's empty mirror, empty of everything but me. In the light of late afternoon, I appeared to be as slight as a reed, "Nothing," in Mother's words, "but a bone." Approaching the mirror, my eyes were drawn to a pencil-thin line that had appeared miraculously from my navel to my sex, my sex which was already in the shadow of a small wing that, in no time at all, would become so black it might have been painted on with ink. Soon I would be a woman, the mirror informed me. I gazed at my body with exhilaration. And then I began to spin before my mother's mirror as a dervish spins before the temple gate. The more I looked, the more I was the mirror's creature; without hesitation I played a deep game. Spinning, I filled the space of Mother's absence with eyes: the many eyes of men. As I danced, I imagined I was the beautiful Dólet-Khâtoon dancing on the blades of knives for Suleymán; I was Jullanar, dancing on the ocean waves; I danced for a host of men, and I danced for Ramses Ragab. My body was so new it was forever; it was so smooth the eye could not catch hold of it but only glide from limb to limb.

"Beauty," Ramses Ragab would say just a few hours later when we shared a steaming brass dish of lamb cooked in onions, as promised, "always challenges God. And this is especially true of the body. Which is why it is forbidden to show the body in the art of Islam. One gazes at a beautiful body, a beautiful face, and forgets to worship Him. One's only wish is to worship the Other, one's lover . . ." Having said this, he breathed deeply, his mind far away. I could not help but think of those tantalizing images, those dizzying configurations: *The Operations of Nature. The Divine Pleasures of Marriage.* Wistful, I toyed with the three glass bracelets I had bought from a street vendor as Father and I crossed the bridge on our way to meet father's friend. They were a deep carnelian, and they circled my wrists like wounds.

"You are wearing the attar of rose I gave you," Ramses Ragab said to me then, "and this fact greatly enhances the evening's charm. Your daughter is charming," he said to Father, who took up my hand and, giving it a squeeze, agreed.

"See how she takes after her father!" he laughed.

"With your permission," Ramses Ragab continued with exaggerated courtesy, "I shall be your eternally enchanted supplier of rose perfume." Unsure how to handle so much attention, I continued to toy with the bracelets at my wrist.

"They are lovely," he said.

"Well . . . they are only *glass.*" I held my wrist out for him to see; my wrist seemed so beautiful now that Ramses Ragab was looking at it. Suddenly I was seized by a fit of laughter. At what? My own extraordinary behavior, I suppose.

Father said:

"Du calme!" But I could not stop laughing. "What have I missed?" he asked—Ramses Ragab was laughing too—"Is the joke on me?"

"Not at all!" Ramses Ragab hastened to reassure him. "It is youthful exuberance only that has your daughter laughing. As for me . . . her laughter is *infectious*. Do you say that? *Infectious?*"

"Your English," Father said, "is impeccable." The next thing he said was: "Sweetheart, where did you get those bracelets? Have I seen them before?"

"But I just bought them on the bridge!" I cried, still laughing, yet perplexed. "Don't you remember?"

"A fine choice," said Ramses Ragab. "Now all you need is a red dress. To be as beautiful as Schéhérazade. You will wear a red dress and fragrance of attar of rose, and you will be among my most cherished clients, more cherished than the daughters of sultans, khaleefahs, and weezers!"

"Who are your clients?" Father asked.

"Who? *Everyone!* The stylish, the frivolous, sirens and sluts, voluptuaries and brides . . . dandies, of course; I see lots of dandies. Anybody game for amorous adventure, coquettes . . . courtesans"—he smiled mysteriously—"I see *all* the creatures of the night. Who have I forgotten? Ah, yes: the enemies of ugliness, ugliness and tears."

"That's some list!" said Father. I noticed he had barely eaten and that his eyes looked tired.

"There's more!" Ramses Ragab said, and all at once I realized that he was trying his best to lighten Father's mood.

It was as though Father were wearing a suit of lead and Ramses Ragab were attempting to undress him. "The weak come to the *Kosmètèrion* also. Those who approach old age with profound embarrassment, who cannot look into the mirror without seeing maggots already feasting on their eyes. They come hoping for a miracle." I was stunned by his words and sat, as was my wont when taken by surprise, with my mouth open.

"There are those who say I dabble in poisons," Ramses Ragab said then with feigned petulance, "but this is a lie, the lies of my rivals: Abbas Hafiz Knittab and Fathi Bey, whose perfumes all smell of baby shampoo!" Taking my lips delicately between his thumb and forefinger, he gently shut my mouth so that I nearly wept with embarrassment.

"At Memphis," Father said, "a fly flew down her throat."

"It is a wonderful thing," Ramses Ragab offered kindly, "to be so easily astonished. It means your soul is quick, Elizabeth. Very quick and nimble!"

"The first time I invited you to play at war," Father said, "our servant, Gamal, threatened to leave. 'I cannot serve in a house into which magicians come and go like cats in an alley!' he said. My wife asked: 'What sort of a magician?' Gamal said: 'He concocts love potions, things with dung, filth like that.' "

Mother was intrigued. The day Ramses Ragab had come for the first time, she had made up her face with lavish attention. She had put on a *gallabeyya* of brocade, and gold sandals, and had stood silently in the doorway of

Father's study until Ramses Ragab looked up. He got to his feet at once.

"Monsieur Ragab," Mother had said, both mocking and seductive, "my servant tells me you are a dangerous magician; my girlfriends say you are some sort of genius." As I looked on from my perch in Father's oversized reading chair, holding my precious copy of *The Arabian Nights* to my heart, Mother shifted her weight from her right hip to the left, charging the air with heat.

Father, on his knees, gazed at her also. "Can you make me a perfume," she asked at last, "unlike any in Cairo?"

"I will make you Susinum," he said. "It was once wildly fashionable in Rome. It is marvelous. It can even be put in wine. No one else knows the secret of its manufacture."

Clearly she liked this response. He intrigued her—most men did—and now, having gotten a good look at him, she liked his looks as well.

"Susinum, then." She smiled. "Don't keep me waiting long." Then she had gone straight to the kitchen, where she sent Gamal packing.

———

Toward the end of the evening, Ramses Ragab offered me "a little introduction to Egypt's lovely hieroglyphs which so enthused Kircher." I have never forgotten the first three signs he sketched with an elegant silver pencil on the back of our menu:

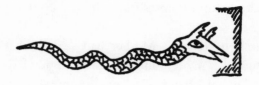

"This is a horned asp going into his little house," Ramses Ragab told me, "and it means *to enter*. Here, the little asp is leaving; it means *to depart*."

"The eye drawn with tears is . . . what else could it be? It is weeping. Whenever you see it, you know that the subject at hand is weeping."

My Mother's Mirror

The following morning Mother's mirror was taken away. Having no vehicle, four men carried it from our house in Zamalek, across the bridge, and nearly all the way to Mother's mysterious new rooms. And if Father and I had not been reading Cairo between the lines, it would not have meant anything at all that the four men—stunned by the sight of a very pink and hairy man named Karl Julius Martens from Kiel, wearing walking shoes the size of tubs, his pear-shaped body strapped to an outsized knapsack, a watch on each of his furry arms—collided into a cart loaded with dung, spilling glass onto the street and badly compromising the mirror's handsome gilt frame. Mother sent the bills to Father—for the carriers' fees and later, for the repairs, and he, out of misguided affection, paid them.

FIVE

On Sympathy

Apparent in the faces of her children, there is a gravitas about Egypt. To appreciate this, go to a museum of ancient history and look into the faces painted on the Egyptian coffins. Look into those eyes thickly rimmed with paint as if with kohl, blue or black. These are the eyes of Ramses Ragab as he turns his face into the light of morning. All at once it seems the time is long ago and I am in a sacred space, the sanctuary of the temple of Heliopolis, or a chapel built of willow wood beside a sacred lake. Turning from the window, he looks at me and the pupils of his eyes grow larger. Were he himself sacred, were he a god of Old Time, he would rule the moon—with those pupils of his that grow smaller and larger!

This morning it seems he is not eager to do battle, although the soldiers are all in their places and the bright dice wait in their deep cup of red leather. The dish of olives is reduced to pits, the bread and cheese to crumbs. We have polished off the pot of jam brought from Fayum, a celestial jam smelling of prodigality, an archaic jam made of roses and honey.

"There is a sympathy," he sighs, "between roses and honey."

"Sympathy?" Father asks, picking his teeth, intrigued. Ramses Ragab tells us that the Universe is webbed with sympathies. That he had chosen the girl, Sakkiet, because *her fingers are in sympathy with the roses of Fayum.*

"This morning she is making rose perfume in the manner of Dioscorides." What, we wonder, does he mean?

"First she will rub her hands with raw honey, next she will toss the roses into green olive oil, finally, with her *sympathetic* fingers, she will stir the petals and slowly crush them." I shiver. I cross my own fingers beneath the table to conjure my jealousy. Sakkiet's sympathy with roses causes a ferrous taste in my mouth—a little like tasting blood. When it had pricked my heart, jealousy had made it bleed.

I am wearing my new glass bracelets. Resting my elbow on the table, I hold my head up with my hand so that the glass shines and color washes over my neck. Feeling the braided glass against my skin, pleasure overtakes me. I am warmed by the promise of my own impending beauty. My darkness a *sympathy* between my father's friend and me.

Not so many months earlier as Mother sat at her mirror battling time she complained: "Why are blondes so fragile? These Egyptian broads go on forever! It's because they're so damned *dark.*" She had looked up and glared briefly at my skin the color of olives, my black hair—before her attention was reclaimed by her pots of cream, her colors, her combs and pencils and powders. (Now, whenever I see the guardians of the dead painted on tombs—and they have the faces of lions and bulls and *asses!*—I think of her witchy pots and jars, her eternal, her hopeful, her desperate idolatry.)

At the height of her powers, Mother had bragged to her best friend, Boduur: *I can have any man I want.* They were sitting together on the verandah of the Sporting Club and a group of Egyptian officers, cocky after the recent successful army coup, were looking their way and laughing. Boduur was shocked. "But . . . Egyptian men are all so easy!" she countered cruelly. This was Mother's word for what Boduur had said: *cruelly.* I asked Mother what Boduur meant by *easy.*

"Boduur is jealous," she explained. "They're all jealous of me, here, in Egypt. Boduur, Fahima—" Laughing at a private joke, she took up a lock of her pale hair and bit into it, as though it were something good to eat.

"But Mother," I forced myself to ask, "isn't it *Father* you love?"

"I'd love him more," Mother began evasively, tearing open a fresh pack of cigarettes, "if—if—" She knocked out a cigarette and continued: "Well! And *so what* if the men are *easy*? All men are easy when faced with a beautiful woman." She struck a match. Nostrils flaring, she snorted: "Easy. And *hard*!"

Yet Boduur had shaken her self-esteem. If the men were easy—and she knew it was true—then how could she be certain of her own *animal magnetism*? That night as she sat before her mirror I heard her sigh:

"And what if it *is* too easy to be wanted in Cairo? What would happen, honey," she purred to her own reflection, her voice thick with smoke and anisette, "if I walked around in sneakers *without my face*? What if"—she leaned into the mirror beaming somewhat boozily at herself—"I just dropped the gold lamé and the petite white suit, huh? What would happen if"—she began to brush her luxurious hair, freshly hennaed and rinsed with chamomile—"I walked around town in a baggy brown dress? What do you think, Lizoo," she asked, as on her bed I sorted her jewelry, separating the gold from the silver in little heaps, "would they be so *easy* then?"

———

The next day an Abyssinian *devin* came to our street. He installed himself in a lost corner where refuse had accumulated, and made a nest of faded rags and dirty straw. As our neighbor's maids had their fortunes read in sand, Mother and I looked on from the kitchen balcony. Snapping beans, Beybars muttered something about *seedy characters*.

"Ah! Beybars!" Mother teased, "stop scolding and come down with us. Everyone wants to know the future!"

"Mush a-iyiz!" Beybars shook his head. "I have the sense in my brains to stay away from crackpots!"

Mother grabbed her purse and a moment later she was waiting in the street for her fortune, perched above the *devin* on gilded hooves, her hand poised on her hip like Rita Hayworth. The *devin* had lashless eyes, and part of his nose had been eaten away by leprosy. He kept Mother waiting a long time.

"Mourn Beauty's loss." He said this suddenly, piercing Mother with his naked eyes, eyes unlike any I had ever seen, red and gold. Impatiently he brushed the sand away, effacing the mark she had made with her hand.

"You!" he said to me. *"It is your time."* He poured fresh sand down at my feet. But Mother was angry and threw a coin down hard, scattering the sand that was meant for me.

———

Back to sympathies. Sympathies and the weeks just following Mother's departure.

I had, on a visit to the museum, seen the sacred hill of Osiris; it looks something like this:

And so, one afternoon, once Ramses Ragab had done playing at war with Father and had returned to the *Kos-*

mètèrion, I drew my own set of sympathies. The hill I drew stood for the *Kosmètèrion.* Within it I drew a bee, the petal of a rose, the eye of Ramses Ragab, my own heart, a sack of sand containing a question mark. The trees planted on the hill were acacias and figs beneath which we had sat, the three of us: Father, Ramses Ragab, and I—eating sweets.

That night, as Father slept, I took a needle from Beybars' sewing kit and with black ink pressed the image—reduced to a sign—into the flesh of my inner arm, a few inches above my wrist:

When a few days later Ramses Ragab would see this he would exclaim:

"Ah! But Lizzie? You have a sacred hill, the sacred grove inked to your skin! How astonishing!" Sitting back and looking at me with deepening interest: "You are a funny one, Lizzie—" hurting me, unintentionally, to the quick. Yet, bending closer, with a troublous, questioning smile, he at once repaired the damage.

"But look!" he said, "your arm is swollen a little." He plucked a piece of ice from his water glass and taking my hand, pressed it to my skin, as down the hall Father whistled a military march and fussed with his troops. "I have *never,*" Ramses Ragab whispered, "heard of a girl giving herself a tattoo. Does your father know?" I shook my head.

"In the desert," he murmured, "it is the old women who tattoo the girls. Here"—he touched my forehead, "here, here"—my cheeks—"and here." He touched my chin. "I like it," he decided. "It's . . . *unanticipated.* Only, don't make a habit of it."

"I won't," I said. "This is magic enough."

"Ah! It's about *magic*! I thought it was about . . ." he hesitated, "raving beauty, I suppose." He grinned. I grinned back and tapped my bracelets against my teeth—a gesture that caused him to look away in confusion. I would be *unanticipated* or nothing at all!

"Ana gehiz!" Father cried from his war zone. "I am ready, General Ragab, to take you on! My horses are snorting fire!"

"Who are you, today?" I asked.

"Darius," he said. "Your father is Alexander the Great. *Who are you?*"

"I'm Lizzie," I said. "I'm *staggering*!"

———

In the States we lived in the country. There was a hill not far from the house I called "Riddle Hill." It stood alone at the far corner of a meadow. Although Mother said the hill was made of all the stones and useless stumps several generations of farmers had discarded in one big heap, Father called it "the tumulus" and insisted it contained a skeleton; perhaps he said this only to excite my imagination. However, the hill's origins interested me less than a vision it had afforded me: the vision of Mother one late afternoon reeling across the meadow—could it have been *in agony*?—to fall to her knees and battle the ground with her fists until she had exhausted herself. Then she had collapsed into the deep grass and slept—or so I think, because she did not move for hours.

I stood on Riddle Hill within the shadows of its trees wanting to go to her, yet too afraid. I imagined it would have been a terrible thing for her to know I had seen her, whereas now I think if I had had the sense to run down the hill and put my arms around her, to press my body close to hers, everything might have come out differently. Yes, now I fear I failed her. That, rather than watch her in silence, I should have given her comfort. But this was impossible because I had perceived something scandalous. I was certain my friends' mothers did not spend the afternoon beating the earth with their fists and sleeping in the grass. An unanswered riddle is a maddening thing and so is a secret that cannot be shared. I felt like a spy the following day and the many days after when, thickened by self-loathing, I returned to Riddle Hill to stand alone and watch for her return. And if there is nothing more solid than a hill crested with boulders and trees, still I stood as in a boat without sails, anchor, or oars, brooding and rocking, spellbound by endless and endlessly mutable interpretations of what I had seen: Mother is mad; Mother is sad; she is eccentric; she has a dark secret. *She is homesick*—at last, a comforting thought! One night I asked her the single question I could manage without provoking her curiosity. *No*, she said. *I hated home. Besides, I was so little. Just a kid when we left.*

From then on the small pleasures of daily life took on the stench—however slight—of ambiguity or worse: *deviance.* And although I loved Father deeply, this secret knowledge revealed what I came to think of as his weakness. Was he blind? Did he not see Mother's despair? Was he unable, unwilling to do anything about it? Was her loneliness so entire, so established that nothing could be done? And then there was the problem of her beauty, her restless beauty, its incessant transformations. (For a time she was so taken with Lucille Ball she shaved her eyebrows and penciled them in; she became a redhead. But the night Father's Chair invited them for dinner to celebrate Father's tenure, Mother was a blonde again, a blonde who had somehow managed to find a gold lamé sheath in the sleepy, wool muffler, rubber boots, and long johns town of West Wilbur.)

———

In those years Father had not yet begun to play at "little wars" although, fascinated by military history, he had undertaken a panoramic investigation he eagerly shared with me, bedtimes. Night after night I was entertained with the riotous militias of Mesopotamia—who fought with bludgeons of brass, the mighty Assyrians—whose iron weapons forged an empire, the mysterious Hyksos—who bellowed the names of their gods as they tore into Egypt on chariots, the howling mercenary armies of Macedonia— "Let the kid go to sleep!" I recall Mother shouting from the TV room on school nights when Father, beside himself with excitement, described the beautifully cuirassed fighters of Rome (and how lovingly he would paint these in years to come!), the fabulous armies of India whose detachments of saffroned elephants he could not help but return to, despite Mother's sighs, supper times. Ah, but . . . India had more to offer! The day Father encountered an enigma called the Poison Damsel, a torch was lit in his imagination and he began to write a book, the book that made him famous, the book that would ensure the Fulbright that got us to Cairo. With the meticulousness of the nascent hobbyist, Father describes practices condemned yet employed by the Romans and the Greeks, vilified in the sacred books of India, perfected by the Dutch, the Spanish, the Hittites, the Vikings, the Germans, the Chinese; the British in Ireland and the New World, the Portuguese in Araby. He describes the manner of poisoning a cup of coffee—popular during the regime of Al Rashid—by inserting arsenic beneath the thumbnail and serving one's guest oneself; the use of lethal tobacco in the Indian wars of North America and poison rum in Tasmania; the horrible exploits of Gaspar de Espinosa in Peru, and the Duke of Alva in the Netherlands; the sterilization of the enemy's seed supply and soil and, looking into the future, the use of "discreet toxins" (Father coined the phrase) that would over time compromise an entire population's immune system and reproductive capacity. (And the Poison Damsel? Ah! She was one who, fed particles of poison throughout her infancy and girlhood, could at maturity *kill with a kiss*!)

The notion of "discreet toxins" turned out to be of special interest to the CIA. Father was invited to Washington to give a series of lectures. His vanity, the chronic loneliness of the college professor abandoned to the trying anonymity of a rural campus of six hundred students and a minuscule endowment, ensured that he would accept with gratitude and kept him from inquiring too deeply into just who had invited him and why. Father's book was titled: *The Ethics of War*. His host in Washington suggested with an eerie laugh it would be better titled: *Depravity: A Manual*.

I recall how Mother—always radiant during dinner parties:

> Learn to put the vitality you waste in head motions
> into your eyes and your voice!

—astonished Father and his guest over coffee and pie ("The one good thing I brought from Iceland is a taste for gooseberry pie!") when, after Father had described his book to Tack Ravan, a colleague in anthropology, Mother piped up:

"Honey. If you dislike war as much as you say, why the heck isn't your book about peace?"

Father looked pained, even bewildered. Tack Ravan, whose special field of inquiry was betel chewing in Pakistan, gazed at Mother with curiosity.

"True!" he agreed, "it is! It would do well to peace. To peace pursue it." Luminous, Mother cut him a second slice of pie, and I saw that his eyes watered as gooseberries swelled and tumbled across his plate. He smiled at Father remorsefully.

"Tell me," Mother asked. "Does your name *mean* something?"

"Ah . . ." With delicacy he prodded his pie, apparently touched and sad. "It means a . . . conveyance. A . . ." he lowered his voice, "traveling throne." When Mother and I burst into laughter, he laughed too, and merrily.

"How wonderful, said Mother, still laughing, "to have a name that is both somehow beautiful and so funny."

"It is so," he said. He smiled at her with gratitude.

"I have teased you terribly." Mother turned to Father. "I mean about your book. I'm a terrible tease," she said to our guest, who was quiet now, watching her. "It's fate, you see. What happens to us girls who grow up *snowbound.*"

———

It occurs to me now that the reason why Father applied for that Fulbright may have had everything to do with his guilt over his brief encounter with the CIA—a way of keeping his distance. I believe his lapse came to trouble him, especially when certain lethal procedures he had made much of during his Washington lectures were used by the United States—and for the first time—in isolated areas of the globe inhabited by tenacious and indigenous peoples, areas rich in resources American companies were eager to exploit. He once received a small bronze medal in the mail for his "services"—a thing he tossed to the floor in a rare display of temper. (Perhaps I have at last solved the mystery of *that* peculiar moment!)

And what of Mother's "snowbound" infancy? Did this, I wondered, somehow explain the *something gone missing* in our lives?

SIX

Grilled Pigeon and Counterpane Wars

Summer was spawning ill temper. I resented everything, above all my own indeterminate age. The morning Mother sent word that I was to meet her at the Sporting Club for lunch, I locked myself in the bathroom, overwhelmed by the homeliness of my own knees. Because Father was busy painting Persians in preparation for war with Ramses Ragab, it was our servant, Beybars, who coaxed me from the bathroom.

I saw her at once. Resplendent in a lemony silk suit, her hair bleached to a new whiteness, her waist anchored by a gold belt, she looked like Mother, only more so. When she saw me, she smiled her impossible diva's smile, a smile I had seen her rehearse, bending into her mirror and breathing the words *abbess, abyss,* and *ablaze.* Mother could say *ache* and *absence* showing all her teeth. As I crossed the interminable floor she gazed at my feet with fascination, her eyes crowded by impatience. Then offering her cheek to be kissed she murmured: *Lizzie, Lizzie, Lizzie.* The air was saturated with the whispering of waiters, the Sporting Club's eternally dribbling piano.

"What's your father up to?" she asked, searching the verandah, perhaps for exits. Aware of her slightest move, two waiters sped forward. She ignored them.

She was wearing a scarab of pale blue faience. It hung from a thin gold chain and settled on her breast bone except when she leaned to adjust a sandal or reach for a cigarette, when it hovered in the air. The scarab made for a very small shadow above the deep cleft of her breasts.

I ignored her question. I knew if I told her that Father was painting Persians, she would toss her fabulous head and snort. She smelled of Susinum. I said: "Are you coming home?" On either side of her, the waiters lingered. They, too, were looking at the scarab's shadow. On her wrists she wore heavy gold bangles, thicker, more numerous, than those I remembered.

"Poor gosling," she smiled ruefully. "To have *such a bad mother.*" She took my breath away. She said, "Let's order lunch. The pigeons are boned and stuffed with something. They grill them. With their heads on!" She laughed. "They're very good." Our waiters bubbled over us in agreement. Before I could respond she had ordered pigeons for the two of us.

"Are you *really* bad?" I asked. The conversation was treacherous, and I felt overwhelmed with something like fear.

"I couldn't be worse." She said it lightly, her eyes skidding, attracting more waiters who, aware of her every tremor, approached. She did not see them. Bending sideways toward the floor, she snapped her purse open and reached for a fresh pack of Sphinx filters. When she lifted her head a flame leapt in readiness. She received it, touching the waiter's cuff with her hand. His face darkened.

"With the pigeons," he asked, gazing into her eyes shamelessly, *"du vin? Une salade?"*

"Mais, oui!" she exhaled. "Just bring whatever goes with them." He stood still, breathing her smoke. "And please stop hovering about, like . . . like . . . They remind me of dirigibles!" she confided. "What's that smell?" Her nostrils quivered. "Is that *you,* Lizzie? Smelling of attar of rose?"

"No," I lied.

"So tell me . . ." She inhaled dreamily and prized a crumb of tobacco from her tongue with her nails. "Why the green socks?" A large bottle of mineral water struck the table then, and a carafe of wine. From across the lawn came the cries of children in the shallow pools. There was a diminutive pool for toddlers, and their voices were especially shrill. A waiter poured her wine, another flourished a large silver dish. "If it weren't for all those damned babies—" Mother killed her cigarette. Grapes in their beaks, the birds were served. They could not have smelled better. I slipped my sandals from my feet and pulled off the green socks discreetly, rolling them into a tight little ball. Mother picked up her knife and fork. When she lifted a bird from its string potato nest and sliced into the breast, I dropped the ball to the floor and kicked it clear across the room. Mother put a neat sliver of meat into her mouth, having glazed it first with its violet sauce, and sighed. Then she ordered a whiskey sour, and then she remembered me. She nodded in the direction of my plate to prod me on.

I had vowed not to eat in order to convey how miserable our lives were, Father's and mine. But the pigeon and its perfumed sauce proved impossible to resist. When I looked up again, Mother was *elsewhere,* her whiskey sour and freshly lit cigarette demanding her full attention. Later I would punish myself for having eaten lunch, for having put up with her silences, for my own inability to entertain her.

As I ate, I wondered what it would be like to be that beautiful. To have the power to set the air ablaze with a simple toss of the head or sideways glance, a glance whose path I followed now as it scorched the faces of Naguib's spanking new navy and army men, the faces of their painted, huffy wives—the faces that Mother (could it really have been *unknowingly?*) was lighting, one by one, like lanterns.

Women were getting up, pressing the creases from the bosoms and bellies of their silk dresses, rising as lightly as they could, although Mother had made them feel as weighty as waterlogged battleships—pampered, souring women stepping precariously to the ladies' room on spindled legs, to put the pieces of their own blasted vanity together again as best they could, having been cruelly, murderously undone by that maddening, dizzying, unstoppable incandescence of my mother's! I watched as, brooding, they returned, having failed utterly, their girded flesh expanding even as they crossed the room, their bottoms defeated, those gloomy bottoms! Mother's presence on that spiffy verandah was a thickening medium that resisted all female progress. When they managed to reach their tables, kicking themselves for having abandoned their quickened men—men who were humming happily to themselves, men who were absent-mindedly caressing their own gleaming moustaches—these unhappy women, burdened by my mother's beauty as if by sacks of camel dung and bricks, women whose day had been ruined, who, as they glowered over cooling plates of roast lamb, considered stabbing their dewy-eyed husbands in the heart with their own forks—these women wished all manner of corruptions upon my mother.

Corruptions of air, diseases of wasting away, pestilences, goblins in the attic, injury; that her skeleton be replaced by that of a goat. These women wished dishonor upon my mother, the spilling of blood, disfiguring surgery—as all the while their men, all Copts (the Sporting Club served liquor) recognized in Mother's body a temple of the Holy Spirit, and that to enter there was to flourish, to be anointed, to be renewed. (Not that her bed was a place in which to *tarry*, mind you!)

Soon I would discover that Cairo was thrashing with a mass of legends about her, the Divine Fact of her Prodigious Beauty, her Appetite for Love that, or so I suppose, marriage to Father and its limitations had revealed to her, but . . . *how long had this been going on?*

"Ah! The musk of a man!" I had once overheard her say to a friend on the phone. "Antelope, bull, lion . . . these Egyptian men, they all—" Seeing me, she had kicked the door shut, leaving me in the dark, bewildered by this bestiary. Bewildered, that is to say, until that afternoon, when Mother, having revealed to the finite universe of the Sporting Club the cosmical action of crossing and uncrossing her legs, the supernatural feat of licking her lips, the untold puissance of her nipples crying out from under her blouse for attention with all the guiltless energy of newborn twins; my mother who, returning from her mysterious moon to an impoverished world, said:

"That Ramses Ragab."

I held my breath and waited. Finally I said:

"What about him?"

"I like him," she said. "He's an elegant guy." She dipped into her purse and pulled out a small gift for me. I recognized the box at once—something from the *Kosmètèrion.* "You know. Kinda loose-boned or something. Don't you think?"

I said, "I'll open this later."

"Sure," she said. Then she bit the inside of her lip.

"What do you mean you *like* him?" I was drunk with—what could it have been? Something like grief. Something like jealousy. "I mean . . . you like him *a lot?* Or just—"

"I don't know *how* I like him," she said, maddeningly. She smiled. "I know *why,* though. Maybe."

"Well, *why,* then?" Over by the bar a waiter was unrolling my green socks with curiosity.

"For one thing, he's not a flirt." I knew this wasn't true. Hadn't he flirted with me? I relaxed, but only a little. "He's gracious, you know. He's fond of my daughter." She laughed. "He's the *gazelle* type of Egyptian male." The whole back of my head was buzzing, and the room was short of air. "Some of them are broad as bulls and some—"

"He's too young for you, Mom! For godsake!"

"Oh, *Lizzie*!" She raised her left eyebrow and gazed at me with intensity. "Too young for me," she said wryly. "Too old for you . . ." She licked her upper lip. I must have blushed then, because she leaned over and caressed my hot cheek with a hand that felt cool, somehow tender. "It's okay, Lizzie," she said. "I'll stay out of your way." She tossed her hair. "He's not the only gazelle in Cairo!"

For this I punished her. I refused to speak another word, refused her temptations, her offer of sorbet, baklava . . . It was she who broke the silence when, as we arrived at Father's gate and I grabbed the handle of the cab door ready for flight, she whispered:

"You're a passionate creature, sweetheart." Then, in a strange voice, a voice I did not recognize, nor could I decipher, "like me." I ran down the path. *I will not,* I thought, *look back.* Suddenly she was beside me and had grabbed my arm. Her hand was firm, gentle.

"I'm sorry," she said. "I've been boorish. A terrible boor, a terrible bore, a terrible whore, really—" I was crying in my mother's arms somehow, crying as though the world had fallen to pieces; perhaps it had.

"Tell your father," she said then, astonishingly, "that I'm . . . what I did was . . . well. Let's face it," she sighed. "I'm bad news." She gave me one last squeeze. "The truth is," she sighed, "they screwed my head on backwards."

"Who?" What was she talking about? How she bewildered me!

"The *storks,* darling. At the baby factory. You know!" She attempted to laugh.

"I'm not a kid of three, Mom!" I shouted, turning from her, moving away fast.

"I know that, honey!" she called after me. "I was just . . . Oh, *what the hell.*" Then she was back in the cab, her white hand sparkling behind the filthy glass, and then she was gone.

———

The Kubri 26 Juillet passes over the Nile from El Zamalek to Boulac and the greater city of Cairo. All day long, street merchants drift across with fresh eggs and fried dough and lettuces and flowers. One afternoon as Father was on his way to Boulac, he cried out softly and pressed his palm to the side of his head. He stumbled and then he fell. Several strangers, all merchants, carried him to a doctor who practiced on Sharia Boulac.

The doctor called it a "Small Event." It is true that after a few days of rest Father was already on the mend, yet his *défaillance* worried us all. Beybars' kitchen was overrun with cucumbers and melons with which he made special drinks from Old Time, drinks *older than Rome.* These he served over crushed ice, his only concession to modernity. He was convinced Father's heart and brain *needed to be cooled.* And Ramses Ragab came every day as usual, to fight "Counterpane Wars" (his term) with Father, who kept to bed *like royalty,* he grinned, showing the gap between his teeth; *just like that dead camel Farouk!*

Father was Amasis, the king of Egypt, and Ramses Ragab Cambyses, the prince of Persia. In honor of his role, Father had trimmed and waxed his beard to a sharp point. I was beginning to realize just how eccentric Father was, and to consider that if these eccentricities were now more in evidence, they *predated Mother's abandonment.* Would Mother have wanted Father more if he had devoted less time to the games that seemed to crowd out everything else? (Even on our trips together to the museum Father was taking copious notes for his campaigns, puzzling over obscurities: Did the Pharaohs go to war in their symbolical crowns and wigs, he wondered? Or did they fight in more practical attire? Would *anyone* go to battle *in a wig*? Unlikely, and yet . . . Without his wig a king would seem less a god, merely mortal. "He would wear his wig and all the rest!" Father decided, only to begin to worry about footwear, the length of a foot soldier's loincloth, the color of a certain banner, a chariot's tassels.)

Sucking an emerald drink from an imported straw, chewing ice, his legs folded beneath him, his fez at a sporting angle, Father in convalescence gazed with satisfaction at the battlefield that stretched out across the counterpane, its rows of soldiers neatly ordered and freshly painted. Ramses Ragab, who participated in Father's folly (but only up to a certain point; his game was marked by irony; for him the wars were "a fancy sort of chess") had brought along tiny replicas of the male sphinxes Amasis, according to Herodotus, had ordered to be made in his honor. There were also a number of little alabaster pyramids Father had procured in a tourist shop the day before his fall. Both armies were rich in chariots.

"If Cambyses proves victorious, these will be toppled over!" Ramses Ragab whispered as Father, considering strategy, tested the keen edge of his beard. He had placed a little lead bull on the Egyptian side. "When in the past Cambyses was victorious," Ramses Ragab continued, his lips so close to my ear the down on my cheek tingled, "a few Egyptian priests fled for the coast under cover of night. They did not stop until they reached India, and this is why the cow is sacred there, even now." I supposed the priests had carried little bulls of lead just like the one on the counterpane, and that they had worshiped these on their way to India at diminutive altars. I imagined that they also carried branches of frankincense and beads of myrrh to burn in doll-sized cups.

According to Kircher, whom Father now read aloud with great seriousness to "set the mood," and to remind himself and his adversary of the tremendous significance of this battle, "nearly all the wisdom of the Egyptians perished here . . . here the old gods were pounded to dust!"

Looking around the room, I wondered where India could possibly be. "Supposing," I offered, "the floor is the sea, the carpet the land. Then India's *there*—" I pointed to a bookcase listing with illustrated books of navy battles. And the priests, where were they? Father pointed to a small temple, the tops of its columns painted a beautiful grass green. "They're in there." "Should the Egyptian army fail," said Ramses Ragab, "you may take them to India yourself, Lizzie, following the contours of the carpet coast."

Apart from the rattling of the dice and my father's occasional battle cries, which brought Beybars running from the kitchen: *"Il est fou! Quoi faire?"* the room was quiet and dappled with sun. I stretched out beneath the window to read my precious *Arabian Nights,* delectating in the words, the closeness of the current king of Persia:

> . . . she was stunned by his beauty; his eyes, so intensely black, wantoning like those of a deer . . . his fragrance diffused itself like the fragrant musk of a deer . . .

"What does it mean," I asked, "his eyes *wantoning*?"

"It means his eyes are roaming," Father said, as with the help of a six-inch ruler he positioned twelve chariots three inches to the left—no easy task as the counterpane was not perfectly flat.

Ramses Ragab said:

"Like a hawk that flies afield and cannot be tamed." He spilled his dice and made a move. Father groaned and leaned back as if in pain.

"You must stop this!" I cried, rising to my feet and tugging at the counterpane so that the little men, the pyramids, and chariots all toppled over. Father raised his hands in horror. "You must stop thinking about her all the time! Do you imagine she ever thinks of you?"

"Don't you see that I'm lost?" he said, one hand pointing at the fallen soldiers, one hand at his heart. "I'm *lost!*" he repeated with astonishment. Meeting his eyes, I saw that it was true. And when I glanced at Ramses Ragab, it seemed that he, too, knew that this was true.

"No!" I said, frightened for the first time, more frightened, even, than when he had returned home with the doctor, an eggler and a poulterer sustaining him, each to a side—"You can't be lost!" Close to tears I stood above him. "Because . . ." I thought for a moment: "Because, if you're lost, that means that I am lost, too." Yet, even as I said this, it seemed that he was fading away, dissolving into the pillows that held him. I walked closer and kissed his face.

"All will be well, Lizzie." Ramses Ragab was standing beside me. With infinite sweetness, he caressed my hair.

"Ma pauvre chérie." Father looked crestfallen. *"D'avoir un père si minable."* He hesitated. "I wasn't always like this." He sighed again, deeply, and then he was asleep. The suddenness with which he fell asleep was profoundly unsettling.

Ramses Ragab and I removed the soldiers, the chariots, the little bull of lead, the temple, the sphinxes, and the pyramids from the counterpane. I remember that Ramses Ragab took up Father's feet to tuck them beneath the covers. That the beauty of my father's feet astonished me.

SEVEN

The Garden of Semblance and Lies

Late this afternoon when I removed the final wrapping, the flesh was so rigid I needed to use an electric saw to open the chest and abdominal cavities. The body was packed with straw and mud and seeds—a mean, hasty job. It had no heart, and the brain, still in place, had been eaten by insects.

The work I do is not appealing, and this is why there are not more of us doing it. Here in Cairo we are four. Day after day the careful illusions of beauty and duration cede beneath our ministrations. What time has damaged, we damage further.

"Nothing survives death," Abbas, my assistant, likes to joke, "except for antiquity." (How often he reminds me of Father!)

Sometimes a mummy is in extraordinary health. Its teeth and braided hair, the nails of its fingers and toes, intact. The skin of the hands and feet may still be stained red with henna. Someone, Abbas or I, will say: "A beautiful mummy."

The mummy of Lady Rai is such a one. She has all her hair, her teeth, her nose and eyebrows and even her breasts, although, to tell the truth, they are as thin and dry as pieces of parchment. Yet one can tell she had been lovely; lovely, too, Queen Tiye with her fine, high cheekbones, delicate mouth, and full head of thick, curly hair. Sometimes a beauty's face has been so overstuffed with padding it has split; the chest so weighted down with gold the bone beneath has cracked. Often the work I do shames me, and many are the nights I miss the young man who, at the end of our affair, said:

"When I first met you, I thought your work was fearless and fascinating. But now it seems to me you are little more than an undertaker. Or worse. At least an undertaker handles fresh corpses."

I said:

"The tedium of death dissolves our most elaborate illusions. This is why it is a challenge, and why it matters to me." I tried to explain to him that when I take up my scissors and saws, death stares me in the face, and I have to fight my demons in order to continue with a steady hand. I persist because I believe there is an answer to be found, a way to live better than I do. I expect this work to reveal to me what it means to be beautiful, what it means to die, what it means to be human when in the end all that remains is a black rag and a fistful of dirty straw. Yet even now I would gladly be loved by the young man who left me for a woman who—if less thoughtful than I (or so I like to pride myself)—had the gift of laughter.

———

It is a curious thing, but suddenly I realize, after all this time, that the summer of Mother's departure, I was both looking for her and fleeing from her and, even more passionately, I was looking for Father who, always elusive, grew more so by the day. It was as if—I realize this now—his *faiblesse,* as he called it, was a new mask he could hide behind, a novel concealment. For if the real world continued to have a hold upon him—he was still coherent and affable—his eccentricities dramatically worsened. And when Ramses Ragab—who hoped to *stimulate* Father only, to awaken an interest in things other than chess or counterpane wars, to strengthen Father's mind and so his resolve, to prolong the intervals between those ominous weeping fits when he could bear Mother's betrayal no longer— brought Father a holy-minded yet licentious work attributed to Khuwárezm called *The Garden of Semblance and Lies,* the effect was the opposite of all expectations.

Ramses Ragab proposed a reading. *Insisted*—so unlike him!—on a reading. Father had no choice but to put his soldiers back in their boxes—a thing he did lingeringly. But finally the last soldier was tucked into the last box and

Father, looking decidedly "pasha" in fez and dressing gown, propped up by every pillow in the house, proclaimed himself "ready to be entertained." Ramses Ragab had a fine voice and an uncanny gift for giving each character a distinctive timbre and manner; he did not sit still but paced around the room as mutable as the mutable Zaki.

The Garden of Semblance and Lies opens with an exposition on natural and deceptive magic: the one depending upon the agency of God, His angels and djinn; the other on perfumes and drugs. Before we knew it, Father and I were swept away by the fabulous story of a villainous student of natural magic who, by trickery (he stays up night after night spying on his old master), discovers the Ism-el-Aazam—the hidden name of God. This gives him absolute power over everything. He explores the bottom of the ocean:

> which, as everyone knows, is beyond the reach of the sun; he counts the coins kept in the merchant's purses; he listens to the modulations of the astronomical bodies; he understands the ponderous arguments of the philosophers; he gazes into the forbidden faces of the Sultan's wives. Free of all constraint, his mind seizes the totality of things. The rules of appearances—known to God only— are known to him, as manifest as lions and the moon, and the fish of the sea.

Suspended upon the single thread of God's mighty name, the student of magic sails through the air. Catching the scent of attar, he follows it into the shadows of a tightly shuttered room where a girl of unutterable beauty lies sleeping. He abducts her and casts a spell upon her so that she awakens to a false dream of love. In the magician's garden, the garden of the title, the girl gives herself passionately and without shame. The author likens this nefarious enchantment to a black pearl locked inside twelve boxes of lead and buried deep in the ground. A perfect thing, yet still as death. *If the girl is enslaved,* the tale continues,

> the magician himself is subjugated by delusion. If he delights in unending passion, his pleasure unceasing; if his mistress is invariably his and her youth and beauty imperishable, still she is a phantom and their love a lie. Hold her [Ramses Ragab breathed,] and you hold a cup that contains no wine, nor even the promise of wine.

"Nor even the promise of wine," mumbled Father.

One night, as the magician holds his beloved tightly folded to his chest and breathes in the unceasing fragrance of her black hair, he dreams he holds a doll made of mud and straw. In his dream he recognizes that his mistress is no more than a figment, and their tryst death itself. He awakens horrified and, looking at the ageless face he has adored throughout the centuries, is shaken by the extent of his own unforgivable duplicity.

He throws himself to their chamber's floor—a floor of polished silver set with nails of gold, and calling out God's secret name begs His forgiveness. To prove his change of heart, he asks God to *take back His name,*

So that I shall know it no longer. So that I shall never have known it. Take back the years I have stolen from you! [the magician cries, his face bathed in tears.] Make it happen that my master shall have died in peace with your name locked away in his heart. Make it happen that my beloved—whom I love more than eternal life—be once more as she was, long ago, peacefully sleeping, undetected in her father's house.

And he whispers the Ism-el-Aazam.

The story ends with the magician reverently burying his aged master. As he returns home with a heavy heart, he sees a girl at her window, gazing at the moon, and is overcome with tenderness. It occurs to him that the moment—so lovely, so ephemeral—has been repeated countless times; indeed, it seems a thousand-thousand faces burn brightly in the moonlight, flickering like moths before his eyes. With his sleeve he brushes away his tears, and when he looks again, the girl is gone. As he continues on his way, restored, just as his beloved has been restored to the flow of time, and despite his fear that he will never see her face again, he moves quickly, surprisingly grateful for the fullness of existence—that brief gift.

"And . . . *does* he see her again?" Father asked.

"I do not know," Ramses Ragab said gently. "For the story ends there."

"The tale reminds me of what it was like to be young," said my father. "What it was like to live out the day, day after day, in a youthful body. What seemed to me then was a perpetually youthful body! I could not imagine that I would ever weaken. Or be this sad. How *agile* I once was, Ram! Yet . . . I did not value it!" He surprised us by knocking on his own skull hard. "This I valued alone! My overstuffed brain!" He grinned horribly, the gap between his teeth somehow indiscreet. I could see that Ramses Ragab was puzzled by his outburst and eager to be on his way. In a moment the two of us, Father and I, were alone.

Father lay back against his pillows and closed his eyes; soon he was deeply asleep. I took up *The Garden of Semblance and Lies* and searched for a passage that had especially thrilled me. It describes how the girl places a knob of ambergris in her navel. Melting, the perfume spills from her belly to the cleft of her sex. The magician and his bride lie down together for the first time, a time that fulfills the illusion of a distinct moment, but is, instead, perpetual, inexhaustible and static. As dusk claimed the room and as my father slept, peacefully dreaming, perhaps, of a time more suited to his heart and mind, I reached for my own cleft and closing my eyes, brought myself slowly, inexorably to pleasure.

———

What follows is painful to recollect. I have said that I had seen how from time to time, Father, sane if eccentric, would be taken over by what I have called *magical* thinking. In other words, he had, ever since Mother's departure, been flirting with magic and now, as he sat in his robe and slippers, soaking up the morning sun, common sense was spirited away and magic came to claim him. It seemed that early on in the story, Father had ceased to listen to Ramses Ragab's wonderful reading, but to instead engage a dangerous hope, to "entertain a folly" as Ramses Ragab would later say. I recall that when Beybars came into the room with Father's breakfast and Father questioned him about the "spiritual and deceptive arts," Beybars, himself superstitious, was attentive and eager to be of service. At first I thought Father's interest was academic only, that the previous evening's reading had kindled his curiosity. It soon became evident, however, that Father was testing the waters. And as I was convincingly engrossed in my books, Father, in an impassioned whisper, dared say what was on his mind.

"Beybars!" he began, "I need your help—*oui! Oui! Mon ami; ton aide*—to resolve a private—it could not be more private—matter. *C'est délicat . . .*" With unusual solemnity, Beybars set the breakfast tray down on Father's knees and stood before him, waiting. *The Arabian Nights* appeared to take up all my attention.

"Might there be a way," Father began, delicately removing the top of his three-minute egg with his knife, "to mend the rupture between the present and the past, the past and the future?"

"The *rupture?*" Beybars wondered.

"*La rupture,*" said Father. "The rift, the break, *la cassure*—" Beybars nodded. "To, for example," Father continued, "seize the void, *l'abime*"—he prodded his egg—"between then and now and now and then!"

"Then and now and now and then," Beybars seemed to sing. He was thoughtful and watched as Father belabored his egg. "My master is wanting a—" Beybars, I am certain of this, glanced my way to assure himself that I was not listening before he uttered the word: *"magician."*

"And that's what magic *does!*" Father agreed with growing excitement. "Or is *supposed* to do. *N'est pas?* Doesn't it? Isn't that so?"

"I do not know, I cannot say." Beybars replied gravely. "I am not an educated man." Father persisted:

"If time is a *fabric . . .*" Father wondered aloud as Beybars hovered above him attempting to decipher Father's intentions, "and if magic"—he glanced at Beybars with intensity—"could drive a nail, yes a *nail* between the fibers"—Beybars nodded gravely—"Well! There is no *reason,*" Father thrust a piece of toast deep into the belly of his egg, "no *reason*—as far as I can see—why one couldn't *pick up the pieces.* One could easily *pick up the pieces* if one could recognize the fabric's general shape. The shape . . ." he chewed carefully, "time takes."

"You are wanting love," Beybars whispered with conviction.

"Yes," Father agreed.

"A magician . . ." Beybars mused.

"A holy man," Father corrected him. "Of superior mind and powers. I do not wish to *harm* anyone. Only—"

"To bring her back?" Beybars sighed, perhaps dismayed.

"Yes." Father agreed. He peppered the last of his egg. "I am wanting her to return. I am wanting the love of the one woman who matters." He said this so softly I could barely hear him.

"A magician . . ." Beybars mused. "Of superior mind and powers . . ."

"Time is a clutter," Father decided, "and it needs to be sorted out. A simple thing, really. I wish to stop the commotion in my head and to set things back on course. The more I think about it, the more I can see what happened."

My nose in my book, I felt my heart stumble. Father closed his eyes and slowly sipped his coffee.

"A misplaced event." Father mused. "A thing that should not have happened. Like a *knot* in the fabric of time, *vois tu.* Surely such a knot can be, could be—"

"Pourquoi pas?" Beybars filled Father's cup.

"Undone," said Father. And then he was sobbing with such violence his tray slipped from his knees to the floor. A second egg rolled under the bed. Father's slippers had sustained most of the damage, and Beybars rushed them to the kitchen sink. As he attempted magic of another kind, I confronted Father.

"It's only a game," he looked haunted, chagrined, "a new sort of game, a game to keep my mind from wandering too far! I *stagnate,* Elizabeth," he attempted to win me over, "I stagnate beneath my fez like a toad beneath a stone."

"But to call for a *magician,* Father! Even as a joke! You've become *stupid*!" I cried, cruelly. "You've always told me how important it is to be *rational* and now you're turning into some sort of *freak* and I hate it!" Seeing him grow pale beneath his bright red fez, I felt ashamed for the two of us.

Father was stunned.

"There is no reason, no reason at all," he began, "Elizabeth! To work yourself into a rage, a rage over a mere exercise in *frivolity,* Lizzie! A small *diversion.* Didn't I just *say* this is all about *diversion*? Indulge me, dearest," he pleaded, looking more and more miserable by the second, "indulge your woebegone papa and allow him this *tout petit divertissement.* After all: *c'est pour rire.*"

"It isn't funny!"

"It amuses me—"

"Then why did you go and cry just now in front of Beybars, Papa! If it's all just a joke?" "Because the joke is on me," he replied, quietly. As so often, his cleverness disarmed me. "Aren't you at all *curious,* Lizzie?" he insisted. "To see *un mage* up close? The *real thing,* sweetheart? Don't say you're not the least bit *curious*!"

I gave in a little and smiled.

"Come," he said, patting a spot beside him on the bed. "Come sit near me so I may look at my beautiful daughter and find peace." But it was our day at the baths together, Mother's and mine; her "man" was at the door and already Beybars was hastening me from the room. I kissed Father and took off.

"Steal a lock of her hair!" he called out with forced merriment. When I glared at him he grinned sheepishly and added: *"Ça pourrait être utile."*

———

"We are constantly shedding skin!" Mother said this with satisfaction. *"This very moment we are shedding skin in this cab!"* Mother turned to me and laughed. I wondered: *What if they are both mad?* and suppressed the thought at once.

"Is that *true*?" I asked.

"Uh-huh!"

What had captured Mother's imagination was not only that we were wheeling our way into dust, but that we were, *she was,* in a state of incessant resurgency. The skin she shed was growing back, and our visit to the *hammám* would accelerate this process. No wonder she was so happy.

"It's like . . . *alchemy*!" Mother cried—a new word of hers. She leaned back, closed her eyes, and moaned voluptuously in anticipation. "You'll see! This is the best part of Egypt!"

A few minutes later we had abandoned our clothes and were making our way into the *hammám*'s athanor. I was struck in the face by a fog of steam so thick it could have been cut with a knife and served on a plate with sauce.

"Just look at them, *dear souls*!" Mother exulted, surrounded by attendants wanting to claim her. Mother, *"la bourgeoise," "la généreuse,"* accepted all available services and tipped well. "Stick with it, Lizoo!" she called before she vaporized on the arm of a beauty seemingly wrought of brass and gold wire. I was grabbed by a near naked matron the size of a small dimpled house. "They've got this *thing* for the body—" Mother's voice echoed in the mist, "the body . . . the body . . ."

That was the last I heard from her for what seemed forever. Alone with my tormentor, broken, reassembled, scrubbed to the bone, I longed for that rent in time Father was so eager to manufacture, that I might fall into it.

Later, when I was left to cool down beside a marble fountain in a crystal air, I stole glances of bodies, vertical and pure; of bodies compromised by ordinary diseases; of lovely, plain, serviceable bodies. And I was among them. The *hammám* had opened its arms to console me. A stranger gently touched my shoulder, and I was offered a cup of tea by an angel whose hennaed hair was the color of carrot cake. I napped, awaking in time to see a girl, like the one in *The Garden of Semblance and Lies,* lift a leg to examine her toe, her sex suddenly visible. The minutes condensed; the seconds passed imperceptibly. And Mother was back, her hair in a towel, her face "as naked as your bottom the day you were born, Liz." She looked like a hothouse plant; she looked like a kid. Somebody you'd see at market in an eternal Europe selling eggs and milk. Radiant, she gave me a squeeze and cried:

"Hey, Lizoo! Whadida say? The world's our oyster!"

EIGHT

On Magic of a Certain Kind

The next morning, Beybars, elegant in a muslin caftan, aroused Father with a plan. He would go to the desert to fetch a magician; he would be gone for a week. He was prepared to leave at once: he flourished a cane, a yellow suitcase, and a pale green train ticket for Nag Hammadi. From there he'd take the *piste* to Aïn el Daker—

"On foot, camel—God alone knows!"

"The middle of nowhere!" cried Father.

"Exactement!" Beybars laughed and, stepping aside, produced his brother Amal, who, girded with a red sash, promised, with great seriousness, to care for Father as he would *the pupil of his own eye.* To prove this, and just as Beybars pulled open the curtains and sunlight poured into the room, Amal spirited a brace of guinea hens from a basket and wagged them triumphantly in the air. So recently had the birds been slaughtered their own eyes gleamed. Father sat up and gazed at the two brothers with amazement.

"An entire week!" he complained. "But, *why?*" Surely you could find someone here in Cairo? I thought Cairo was swarming with magicians. You yourself, Beybars, just yesterday, told me there are as many magicians in Cairo as there are bees!"

"Snake charmers." Beybars scowled. "Jugglers."

"They know how to tumble through hoops and eat fire," Amal said, "but not how to bring back a woman."

"This is a woman," Beybars frowned, "with all due respect," he bowed at Father, "who will be hard to bring back."

"A woman of such evanescence," Father mused, "I wonder at times if she was ever truly *here.*"

With a flurry of feathers, Amal tucked the hens in the basket and withdrew a prodigious string of country onions.

"I am a better cook than my brother," Amal said. "The hens I fattened on barley. They pecked at fat white grubs among the clean stones and metal scraps fallen from the planets. I will stuff them with barley"—he pulled a second basket from the first to prove this claim, insisting that Father take a good look inside—"and lamb sausage." He wiggled his eyebrows suggestively. "These things"—the sausages were now displayed—"will exert a harmonious influence on your mind. I say this with humility." He bowed, then waved a bouquet of thyme in the air.

"In the desert," Beybars confided, "entire countries shift about in the wind. Settlements vanish in the night. The sands walk; the wind speaks!"

"The destinies of men are ruled by the wind." Amal

said this with conviction. "Only the magicians of the desert know how to invoke and how to direct the powers of the wind." He held the thyme to his nose and breathed deeply. "From the village," he said.

"And the *moon*!" Beybars seemed to sing. "The eye of Horus . . ." He spoke so softly it was difficult to hear him.

"The moon?" Father sat attentively as Beybars opened his suitcase and slipped the green ticket inside. The scent of spicy food filled the air. "Meatballs." Father guessed aloud. "Meatballs and the moon—these could fill a life . . ."

"The moon seeds the desert with Powers," said Beybars. Father gazed at the two brothers with fascination.

"You're telling me," he breathed, "that the phantasmic age is not over!"

"It's the Old Magic," Beybars agreed.

"The only magic," Amal added, "that is true."

"It's a leap in the dark," Father murmured. "The odds are long." With a fine brush, he poked the dust from beneath the armpits of a soldier. "Ah! Lizzie!" He grinned somewhat tentatively, I thought, as I came into the room. "This is Amal, Beybars' brother. He plans to look after us while Beybars—and Beybars insists upon it, already has his ticket—" Beybars retrieved the ticket and handed it to me solemnly as proof.

"My brother told me of the young lady," Amal bowed deeply. "And that she has one grey eye and one that is green. I did not believe him, but it is true." He reached into his basket and handed me a small package. "And that she is partial to sweets." Because I had been listening outside the door, I refused to be charmed and did not accept the gift graciously.

"I will roast the little birds now," Amal decided, "and many other tasty grubbery." The two brothers vanished, and a moment later we could hear the cranking of the coffee mill.

"Beybars intends to find a magician of the Old School, Lizzie. The rules of the game have changed and the outcome is undecided."

"Fat chance she'll come back!" I snorted.

"She snorts, too," Father said sadly.

"That's not fair," I said. "I'm not anything like her!"

"Where's your sense of humor, Lizzie?" he asked, the little heap of dusted soldiers growing moment by moment. "Your sense of play? Think of it as an exercise of the imagination. It will be like spending time with a dodo! Or a dinosaur!" The bed was strewn with the impedimenta of Father's parallel universe: tiddlywinks, Tyrolean villages pressed like crackers into boxes, gorgeous ruby-colored dice.

"What if—" he began, his eyes taking on a particularly vague expression I recognized with a sinking heart, "What if the Accidental Universe—which we know to be ruled by aberrant laws—reckless, contrarious, shoddy—*and* riddled with loopholes, is held together, if barely, with *exotic knots*?" As I looked at him it seemed he was caught up in some kind of self-generated weather, a haze so thick I could do nothing but wait for it to dissolve. "What if the Old Magic is part of the fabric? And has an influence on the forces *that sparkle in the tatters like fireflies*?"

When I was a small child, Father would tell me stories about a "cosmic family" who inhabited the stellar regions of a distant galaxy. I wondered if this fantastical venture was somehow a continuation of those stories. If we were the "cosmic family," then the answer to our dilemma could well be found in the stars.

Amal was back carrying the coffee tray and trailed by Beybars. They were talking about *certain things,* the connection between *certain things, lost love,* and—

"What things?" I wondered aloud.

"Little stones that look like fingers, or toes, or ears, and even elbows and knees—"

"There are entire limbs in the desert!" said Beybars.

"Stones with faces." Amal handed me my cup. "Stones that look like the human heart!"

"Fossils," I said. "Father! They're talking about fossils."

"Sacred things," said Amal, "fallen from the sky."

"There are mysteries beyond reason—" Beybars began, clearly miffed,

"Mysteries that deserve our fear," said Amal.

"And our *respect.*" For the first time Beybars glared at me.

"Elizabeth," Father whispered, "it is not like you to be so rude." Amal and Beybars pretended they had not heard. "If the path is strewn with false hopes, I will find out soon enough. We're in *Egypt*," he added, out of the blue, as if this were reason enough, "not West Wilbur!"

"The desert is unlike any other place," Amal said softly. "There even the stones are sexed." I felt dizzy. Ramses Ragab might have said such a thing.

Father asked: "What do you say?"

I looked at the three of them. Father rife with expectancy, Beybars crestfallen, Amal tenaciously amiable.

"I must go to the train—" Beybars hesitated. "If it is your wish, sir. Miss?" He pressed the ticket to his palm and attempted to flatten it. "I am wondering what to do," he added, looking at me. "I am wondering what it is you wish." Clearly miserable, he looked at the floor.

"Godspeed!" Father waved him on. "Already I can hear the wheel of fortune turning!"

———

That day Father got up for the first time in weeks. He spent the morning putting his room in order and catching up with correspondence. He lost an hour looking for a diminutive pair of barbells, and once he had found these exhausted himself within minutes. He took a nap, he took a bath, he trimmed his moustache, and by the time Ramses Ragab had joined us for lunch—the birds stuffed to indecency and poised like swimmers on a swell of spiced lentils, the pickles cut into the shapes of stars and crescent moons, hot unleavened bread and a pudding like a slice of the most ethereal flesh imaginable—Father was, or so it seemed, *on the mend.*

"Let's invent a game," he proposed to Ramses Ragab, "in which magic plays a part." He ignored me when I groaned, and for well over an hour the two of them spoke about the role of magic in war: of Nazi astrologers; of the spell casters who marched with the armies of Babylon; of warrior kings who probed basins of rainwater for the names of traitors; of felt vests soaked in vinegar and impervious to arrows; of inebriated elephants charging with their ears painted red, white, and blue; of shirts woven of devils, and relics tucked into the pommels of swords—a tooth, a lock of hair, dried blood; how Pope Leo III had written a book of charms to protect the soldier from catapults; how the Etruscans foretold victory or defeat in the livers of dead sheep. I could tell there would be no game that afternoon, but a second nap, instead. After lunch Ramses Ragab would return to the *Kosmètèrion.*

Father was distracted, so eager to get down on all fours he forgot to eat and then, when he did, his voracity was boundless.

"Nothing awakens the appetite like talk of war and the follies of others!" he proclaimed with exaggerated pomposity. He reduced his plate to bones, sucked these clean of marrow, downed two more helpings of stuffing and a heaping dish of dessert. Radiant with success, Amal poured water, lemonade, watered the plants, hovered about.

"The birds are too beautiful to eat . . ." Ramses Ragab

sighed, "but still . . ." He accepted a *bit more breast*. He ate with his usual delicacy, a delicacy I tried to match.

"Is it true," I asked Ramses Ragab, thrilled with myself, "that the stones in the desert are *sexed*?" In the street someone played a flute, someone hawked Soviet watering cans. An angel, then another, passed.

"Who told you that?"

"It was I." Amal bowed beside Ramses Ragab's ear. He looked worried.

"Beybars has gone to the desert to find a magician." To give myself courage, I pinched myself hard. "To bring back Mother." Ramses Ragab, the gazelle man, the fastidious eater, pressed his napkin to his lips and answering my question said:

"If they are *strange* enough."

"Strange enough?"

"Well . . . it all goes back to Osiris, you know. His scattered limbs . . ."

"His lost phallus." I had shocked Amal, who backed away and was swallowed by the kitchen.

He milled the coffee with a vengeance. Apparently it was all right for men to talk about sexed stones, but not for girls.

"If the stones are strange enough," Ramses Ragab persisted—and I think he was, in fact, amused, "they were placed in tombs, or used in the manufacture of mummies. They were offered to the gods—as a kind of food—so that the gods would thrive."

"Is the magic of the desert like that?"

"They say that the miners who dig for copper and turquoise still venerate Hathor. They paint her picture on the doors of their houses: a cow with the moon held between her horns. It is she who has seeded the Earth with treasures, you see. Even in the Fayum the healers evoke Osiris when they wish to quicken the blood of those who are sick or dying, or to quicken the sap of trees."

"Father needs some quickening." I said this softly, for he was nodding off.

"So you see"—Father started, opening his eyes very wide and suppressing a yawn—"it shall all turn out for the best. I am eager to share my humble abode with the Old Gods for a brief time. I imagine they need *quickening* as much as I do!"

"Ah! But they are kept on their toes," said Ramses Ragab. "You'd be surprised how fit they are. Rather like your movie stars. The Old Gods are ageless!"

"The child is an American," Ramses Ragab reminded Amal just as he was leaving and as Father tottered back to bed.

"Alors, c'est bien." Amal said this solemnly, as yet unable to look me in the eye.

NINE

Mother Conjured

One week later, Beybars' magician was spirited into our lives. To tell the truth, I have never fully recovered from my initial astonishment.

He was impressive, the tallest man Father and I had ever seen; Amal, too, could not tear his eyes away. His face, burned black by the deep desert and stained with indigo, was made darker still by a blue cloth he wore corded to his hair. He brought the Old Time along with him, along with his own food—dates and clarified camel's butter he melted ceremoniously in a little brass bowl over a diminutive gas burner, and into which he dipped his dates one by one. He also nibbled locusts. He was handsome, although his right eye had been *pruned from his skull by a hawk* (Beybars). He smelled like cold sand. He refused to tell us his name.

And he refused with such authority to share in our meals or sleep in a bed that his simple ways somehow shamed us, and I, too, wished to live on dates and butter, an occasional locust and tea, to sleep on the kitchen balcony beneath the stars. He had a horror of electricity and at sundown retired to the balcony, his eye tucked safely within the shadows of his *haik,* although he confided to Beybars he longed to see the cinema star Fernandel, about whom he had heard so much. Had Beybars seen Fernandel? Was the man's rubber face worth the risks of electrocution? Of having one's bones reduced to paste? And if he insisted that nothing in this world is tangible, he asked to be paid for his services with a live goat. The goat was brought; it slept beside him, Beybars spiriting away its droppings as they fell.

His idle time he spent singing so that the few days he lived with us—he believed the number six was the most productive and so stayed six days—were saturated with sound. I recall awakening from eerie dreams to the magician's singular songs, deeply mouthed and measured, that always coincided with the waking of the birds. Living with a magician was disorienting, yet when he left I was sorry to see him go and watched his impossibly upright figure from Father's bedroom window until he vanished from sight, searching for one final glimpse of him until my eyes ached.

He left charms by my door each evening: a red bead, a blue bead, a green and black coin; and it seemed to me that by accepting these gifts, I was promising him something, although I cannot say what. That I would devote my life to Egypt and her mysteries? Perhaps. Yet were he to see me plucking the bright scarabs from the meticulous linens of his ancestors' corpses, how he would curse me!

Amazingly, Beybars' magician did not speak of *efreets* or djinn or ghouls or prod Father with phallic stones but instead unthreaded all our expectations with poetic flights of mind that endeared him to us unexpectedly. I recall how he once told us earnestly, his voice rising and falling like the impossible piping of a chimera, that mirages are formed by longing, the longing of unwed girls. "The more vivid the mirage," he said (or, at least, this is how Beybars, sometimes Amal, interpreted this speech), "the more passionate the dreamer. Here is one to cause a mirage unlike any other!" he laughed, his teeth impossibly white in the blue of his face as with his one dazzling eye he searched my own. Shaking his head, repeating: "Unlike any other!"

"Lizzie is too young for such dreaming," Father said with tenderness. "Tell the magician," Father requested of Beybars, "that in her own country, she is still too young to be thinking of bridegrooms."

"But she is not *in* her country." The magician frowned. "She is in Egypt and her time is upon her." That phrase again!

———

When Beybars ushered the magician into Father's room, I was looking out the window. In the street below, a blue rooster had just lost its head. Stretched out across the counterpane, Father experimented with a game involving the hazards and enchantments of red dice. Startled by the sudden intrusion, he leapt into his dressing gown as Beybars' marvelous magician bowed so deeply as to touch his knees with his nose. Lifting his face, he gazed, stupefied, by so many men reduced by necromancy to the size of little boys' thumbs. He reached out, grabbed a soldier, broke off its head, and when he saw that it was hollow, laughed at his own foolishness. Father laughed too. Then the magician saw me and smiled. Outside, the sherbet seller's cymbals punctuated the hour. Somewhere, someone was beating a drum.

"Tell your master to remove all these toys," the magician said to Beybars, "but not the dice." His one eye blazed briefly with such cupidity Father scooped up the dice and handed them over. In an instant they vanished inside the magician's voluminous *haik*.

"Tell your master," the magician continued, "that I have come to untie the knot that vexes his tranquility." *Knots!* In his confusion, Father began to hum. "Tell him he must not eat any corpses for the next six days—not of beasts, nor birds, nor fishes." His nostrils twitched. "He smells of chalk. Of old stone walls succumbing to humidity. He is not well."

He looked about the room—we all did—following the gaze of that one fantastic eye. He seemed bewildered by the clutter: the cabinets of soldiers, the cabinets of books, the paints and varnishes, the thinners, the boxes of powdered grass, the islands of *papier-mâché,* the camel saddles piled high with charts and maps, Father's collection of swords, a plumed hat, a fancy leather fly swatter. Meanwhile, the knife and scissors man had installed himself down the street; I could hear the sound of his wheel, grinding.

"Tell your master," the magician said to Beybars, "that it would be better to leave his shop for a quieter room." And he confided to Amal: "Magic and commerce do not mix." Amal explained that Father was not a shopkeeper, but that the room was his bedroom. "The quietest," Beybars hastened to add, "in the house."

"Where does your master keep his camels?" the magician wanted to know.

"He has no camels," Beybars said.

"Only people from another place," the magician grinned, "would have so many saddles and *no camels!*" He laughed until he wept. His laughter was like water tugging at stones. "Let us clear a space, then," he said finally, "for thinking." Beybars and his brother cleared the bed of soldiers and the center of the room of books. When they were done, the magician sat down on the floor and nodding in my direction said:

"The little female may stay as long as she is silent, as silent as a stone at the bottom of a well." An ominous request I thought, yet he smiled at me and nodded as though my presence appealed to him. The two brothers left us to prepare tea, "for the day demands quantities and quantities of tea," the magician said. Once the tea was brought, the magical proceedings began.

I have to say that despite myself, the strangeness of the situation appealed to me: the camel saddles, maps, and books all pushed against the walls, Father regal in bed, his fez on and moustache freshly waxed, the magician pooled in indigo on the floor, Beybars frowning for all he was worth in the effort of translation, Amal in and out with fresh trays of tea, the shadows persistent as the day deepened.

Father wondered if the magician would ask for the assistance of djinn.

"Djinn," said our magician smartly, "with their faces of donkeys and dogs, are only the Old Gods who, over time, have dwindled in the minds of lesser men."

From the depths of my well I saw that Father's eyes twinkled.

"Then it is the Old Gods themselves who will assist you?" Clearly Father relished the idea.

"The Old Gods persist," the magician spoke with reverence. "Their powers persist." He caressed the air as though it were hung with threads and tassels. "These powers," he said so softly that Beybars had to lean closer, "are waiting to be borrowed by those who know the measure of their serviceability. These powers emerge from the whole, are used, then return to the whole. They are never diminished." Father, on his throne, flushed pink. He looked at me with relief, although it had not occurred to me to disrupt the proceedings; they were far too extraordinary.

"Fools believe that magic will revenge them or reveal the hiding places of jars of coins and even the secret of immortal life. The truth is the gods do not concern themselves with enchanted daggers or riches or the coward's fear of death." Having said this, Beybars' magician chose to be silent and for a time the only sounds in the room came from the street below—the dull racket of the fruit seller's cartwheels, the distant grinding of the knife and scissor sharpener's stone. All the world's fragments were swept up and away by that stone, those wheels, and I, at the bottom of my well, began to spin, shedding fingers, elbows, and ears. Tucked into myself, my nose, my arms and legs all smoothed away, I was a sphere spinning into sleep, spinning in a cloud of moonlight, stardust, and sand. Within a haze I seemed to hear, as I descended and rebounded, but so slowly! in my well: *Whenever a man longs for a woman, all he needs to do to cure himself of this affliction . . . is to remember . . . in no time, in no time at all; is to remember . . . in an instant, a brief instant . . . the time it takes for a spark to leap from the fire . . . the time it takes to tie a simple knot . . . She will be, what will she be? A corpse . . . and her face a mask of beetles! A mask of worms, of wasps, of bees!*

My well was full of bees, the drones of wasps; high above me, vultures circled in the air. In my dream I was a piece of fruit, red and orange. An apricot rotting away, roiling with worms . . . *No better than the body of a dead fish fallen to the dust beneath the merchant's stall . . . At first the stench infects the air, but in time not a trace remains . . . not a trace remains to trouble the mind. A woman . . .*

When a crier stood just under Father's bedroom window calling: *Mishmish! Mishmish!* I tumbled fully awake into the final moments of the first day. Late morning was now late afternoon.

"A woman is like this." I peered out over the lip of my well to see Father swamped by bedclothes, gazing at Beybars' magician, deep in a dream of his own.

"Between the instant of birth and the instant of death is an *imposition,* capricious, yet as steadfast in its own purpose as the sun. It joins these irreconcilables, keeps the wayward spirit locked in perpetual confusion, confounds the wise, destroys the weak, and is the root of all noise. Pay heed: the emergency of which I speak is the desire to copulate."

"Ah!" Beybars cried, "it is true! The world and its racket would not exist without the imperious need to—"

"Scarabs." Amal offered as he poured the day's final round of tea. "Cats. Spiders, too! Parrots! All these are impelled to come together!"

"A sticky net," the magician approved. "I have pondered this all my life, yet how simple is the truth."

"Forgive me," said Father. He had taken off his fez and was gazing into it as if it were a pool of water. "I don't see how all this . . . I wonder where . . . How does this affect *me?*" he managed at last. "You see," he said, almost apologetically, "although I understand your point—which is an ancient one and venerable, even ubiquitous—I persist in wanting to see flesh where there is flesh and not pretend there are worms where there are none. The body is fragile," he admitted, "but—"

"A fabric of scabs," the magician insisted, "held together with smoke and the excrement of—"

"Yes!" said Father. "And that is why, you see, it is so precious. The body is—"

"You do not need a magician to tell you that the atmosphere that surrounds lovers burns with sparks." The magician touched the air as though it were alive with flames. "The woman who left was a cinder in the eye; a cinder in the eye is what she will always be." He said this with conviction. "The house is full of her; hot with her heat, tethered with her perfume." He wrinkled his fabulous nose. "An ancient perfume . . ."

He lifted a single blond hair from the carpet and held it up to his one eye. It hung there with an uncanny glimmer.

"One word and she shall be banished by the winds forever. One word and she shall be hastened here."

"What do you think, Lizzie?" Father asked.

"This is your move, Papa," I said as quietly as I could, "not mine." Hopelessly faustisized, Father said:

"Bring her back." The magician considered Father's request before speaking.

"Begging your pardon for what he has just told me," said Beybars, "and what I am about to say."

"Say it," said Father, looking pale.

"He says: 'This wife of his is a terrible nuisance. Why doesn't he divorce her? Because when she returns she'll be disheveled and riding the wind. She'll fill the house with her laughter and the smell of Susinum—' "

"I'd like her back," said Father. "Nevertheless."

"The Universe is full of holes," the magician said, "and this is in our favor." He was pensive once again. "Two is an imperfect number," he declared. "A troublesome number. It designates lovers, and lovers are always in trouble, sooner or later." (But we were not two! We were *three*! What was I, then? The trinity's invisible Dove, brooding in silence and alone; brooding over chaos, alone?)

"We are *three*," I said as fiercely as I was able. "Three."

"This is so!" the magician cried in a sudden fit of enthusiasm. "And three is exactly half of six!" Indulgent, he now allowed me to join the company of men. The deep well of silence was not mentioned again.

———

Over the years I have opened countless spelled boxes scaled with charms and seeded with amulets. The corpse was meant to revive, to acquire the fragrancy of youth, to smell of myrrh and flowering lotus. To stand and step lightly into the next world as one steps from a dark room into a summer's morning. Countless times, I have seen how absolutely magic fails.

And yet . . . how to explain that the next morning when I awoke and went into the living room, the Shiraz was a mosaic of living bumblebees? That when I walked to the balcony to greet the magician and bring him his tea, his eyes were studded with Father's appropriated dice, blood red and marked by a white dot?

How to explain the quantity of serpents Beybars' magician pulled from the air? Serpents as transparent as amber, their visible hearts beating, their viscera like mercury? Or the wind that tore into Father's room suddenly, causing his fez to fly off and hit the wall? How to explain the gold scorpion that hung suspended above Father's head from a strand of my mother's hair? And which broke between his fingers and fell to the floor in sparks? Or the sound of willows thrashing their branches in water, or the bitter taste of gall on our tongues? The taste of honey?

The second day the magician drew magic squares on our open palms and filled them with ink. He asked us to tell him what we saw, however fleetingly, moving there. I saw a flock of birds flying into the mouth of the moon. Father saw a heart studded with nails. On the third day he told Father that the Universe was affected by "desirous" or "desiring" particles. (Beybars could not decide which and was heard muttering: *desirous, desiring; desirous, desiring* for the rest of the afternoon.) He asked Father to write Mother's name on a piece of paper and float it in his cup of tea until the ink had dissolved. His system of sympathies extended and illuminated Ramses Ragab's own. An example: On the fourth day he told us that the leaves of willows have two distinct faces—one turned to the sun and one netted with lines like a human hand. He insisted that everything is legible, including tempers and semen and silence. The kindest thing he said to me—and this on the evening of the fifth day—was: "May your Book of Life always be easy to read." A phrase that currently has me attempting to answer any number of questions such as: *Why, if I have devoted my life to science, have I chosen the most magical of peoples to study and their most magical artifact? Why has love, if it has on occasion chosen to visit me, never chosen to stay?* For I am older now than Mother was when, on the morning of the sixth day, she stood on the threshold for the first time all summer and rang the bell. When he saw her, Beybars let out a cry so strange it brought Father, Amal, and me all running into the hall.

"I was at the Café Fichâoui . . ." Mother began, looking sleepy and perplexed. "I was there all night—such music! Such talk! Which is why . . ." she tugged at the scarlet hem of her suit, checked the deep neckline of her yellow blouse, and began to unravel an emerald green scarf from her neck ". . . I'm so untidy! But I thought—"

It was thrilling to see her, *à l'improviste;* she looked mysterious, elegantly frayed around the edges, exotic, her tired eyes beautiful. In the shadow of the front hall her hair gleamed like very old brass. She looked like Cairo; was taking on its patina.

"I thought—"

We all gazed at her, Beybars with mouth open, Amal with admiration, Father irretrievably amorous. (But where was the magician? He and the goat had vanished. Did he think he had succeeded? Had he known that he would fail? Running to the window, I, alone, saw his departure.)

TEN

La Grande Divinité

If it is true that there are times when my work causes me to feel shame, today I stand by those hours I dare explore the body's labyrinth, its loopholes and portholes and thunder-tubes—and this despite the roaring of the Minotaur.

"Why?" a young man asked me once, a handsome young man I loved, "why have you chosen to spend your life among shadows?" This happened before he left with a woman who knew how to laugh. That woman I mentioned earlier who had the gift of laughter.

"My girlhood was spent with people who mystified me," I told him. "Now I pass my days with those who can conceal nothing." I was attempting levity. "I am a surgical anatomist," I reminded him, "for heaven's sake!"

"I know that," he said. "How could I forget *that*?" It shocked him that I saw the sexes of the dead. "It is true," I said, not taking his dismay seriously enough, perhaps, "I see people's bodies. Not the bodies of angels!"

His eyes darkened. From experience I knew he was closed against me. My heart grew very small. Already missing him I recalled his body's scent of winter pears. His taste of pears. He said: "Don't you see that the dead conceal *everything*? It means nothing to hold a bone in the hand. *Nothing*, Elizabeth." This was the last time I heard him say my name.

"The good thing about the dead," I countered, attempting to amuse him somehow, to detain him if only for a moment, "is that they have already vanished. I mean to say"—I could see the shadow of his hand on the door—*"they can't pull a fast one."* Even then I knew I had lost him.

He turned, moving in that graceful way he had, his grace shattering my heart. There was nothing I could do to detain him. My own, no more my own, gazelle man.

I watched him hungrily, wanting to keep the way he moved within me, the ease with which he moved away, so self-contained, as though not a particle of me clung to him. As though I had never clung to him, or he to me. He walked away as beneath a cleansing rain, as if a rare, violent rain were washing him clean of my nefarious influence, my dark, my dismal, my *dubious* influence! I lifted my fingers to my face to smell them because I thought for the first time (and too late!) that my fingers must smell of the terrible and wonderful things the priests of Old Time had used to secure dead bodies from the horrors of the grave.

"The dead," I said then, following him out the door, "the dead take on the form of a bird. A bird that flies to a tall tree to perch among the gods and eat the fruit of eternal life. *Saleh!*" I called his name. "Saleh! Don't you remember?" I would never speak his name aloud again. "Don't you see"—I'm afraid I was pleading—"the *beauty* in all this?" I attempted a smile, but my lips were trembling.

He said:

"The world has turned a thousand-thousand times since people believed such foolishness!"

I said:

"Please."

"It is the *present time* I love," he told me. "Not the 'Old Time.' I am not interested in your stories of the dead. It is the living I love." He hesitated. "I am no longer in love with you." It was as if he had killed me.

Saleh. The one who, when we stood together in the shadows of the great temple of Karnak, struck the stone with his fist and said: "What Egypt has given the world that matters is not all this, but an extraordinary *idea.* The idea that God created the world not with his hands but with his *voice.*"

Saleh. The one who touched my wrist with tenderness, that place riddled with scars, and asked me *why?*

"Because of one summer," I told him. "The summer of my thirteenth year. Here. In Cairo."

When Saleh left, I was twenty-six, a Cairene again after a thirteen years' absence. I stayed because there was a place for me and because the work of an anatomist is relentlessly exacting. I divided my days between the medical school and the museum, soothed by the work's incessant demand for vigilance. I stayed in Cairo because no people ever cherished the body as much as the Egyptians had, or dared investigate it so fearlessly and with such artistry. I stayed because of the past.

———

Now I will tell you what happened the day Mother appeared conjured by Old Time magic. Thickening the air with swelter—just as we'd been warned—she surged past a speechless Beybars and nearly collided with Father who, in dressing gown and fez, could not have stared at her with more astonishment had she been a sphinx spitting fire— which in a way she was.

"Look at you! A regular-type pasha! And so late in the morning!" She did not know how sick he'd been. I had kept it from her thinking his *faiblesse* shameful, not wanting to give her any satisfaction. Yet I had hoped that someone would let her know how much he suffered. How *elongate* (to use a word of Father's); how *elongate* her orbit had become, yet here she was, on the sixth day, real as summer, in the house she had shared with Father; here she was scenting the air, stirring things up, shedding threads of yellow hair—my lavish, dentilabial mother! Imagine a perfume called: *Accomplished Courtesan*. Imagine a perfume called: *Lashes. Those Delicate Ribs . . .*

"You've returned!" Father was incredulous. He took off his fez and toyed with the tassel.

"Don't be silly," she said. "Besides, you can't possibly want me back." She stepped closer. "Sweet, foolish, *foolish* man!" She reached out and traced the line of his jaw with her finger. "Lean as a rake," she said. "Hey, Liz!" Shyly she gave me a quick squeeze. "How about breakfast with the Whore of Babylon? *Please* don't refuse." I was as much startled by her arrival as that staggering capacity of hers to reinvent herself. What was she wearing? Yellow silk! Scarlet linen! Even the bones of her hips shimmered. She smelled of smoke and anisette. I was enraged with her. How dare she confront Father (and this was a favorite expression of hers) *looking like a million bucks*? *"La grande divinité,"* Father once jokingly called her, the gap between his teeth the size of a tomb. I could see why.

"Keep back those burning arrows, Lizzie," she said, referring to my dark look. It occurred to me that she was a little drunk. "I'm muzzled, myself." *Muzzled?* "Besides, it's rude to refuse an offer of food from your mother." I saw that if her face was open and friendly, *la grande divinité* was poised for flight. I said, "Okay," and thought, incongruously, *keeper of my heart.* Why was I so afraid?

Father spoke up:

"Why not have breakfast here?" A moment passed as he continued to worry the tassel between his fingers in an attempt to compose himself. "Why not?" With a boyish gesture he tossed the fez onto the sofa in the living room. "We were just about to sit down."

"Please, madame!" Beybars nodded, still looking thunderstruck.

Leggy and unpredictable, Mother smiled. She accepted, only, I believe, to bask for a while in the green flames of Father's thwarted love for her and, perhaps, to prove to me just how amiable she could be. Ecstatic, Beybars could not get enough of the miracle provoked by his agency; when after breakfast she departed (with me for the day) and did not return, his disappointment and humiliation were as deep as Father's. Having caught a glimpse of her, Amal, too, was sad. As for the magician, he had atomized. (Or dropped into the street from the kitchen balcony to return to the winds and sands of Old Time else he be blamed for his inadequacies.)

What did they talk about, Mother and Father? To tell the truth, I was so deeply distressed by the hour's sham marriage I cannot say; I poked at my food with my little spoon like a much smaller girl and looked on as Father pilfered glances at her, drinking in the precious instants. There we were, our entire family of three, just half of six, *down to the bone,* the precariously maneuvered separation of our spheres horribly collapsed. Oblivious to the drifts and swells of their conversation, I searched her face for clues but she was as impenetrable as ever. Looking for mischief, I was confronted by her sweetness. Whereas Father could be read like an open book, his eyes brimming his distress, his hope, his hopelessness. From time to time he appeared to be on the verge of tears, but then Mother would say something to make him laugh—such as when she complimented Beybars on his skills in the kitchen, implying more personal proficiencies. This should have shocked our decorous cook, yet so clever was Mother at navigating the troubled waters of sexual innuendo with a seeming lightness of heart, a seeming innocence, Beybars, too, was faustisized.

The magician was right, of course. Mother had returned only to demonstrate once again her *intrinsic effumability* (Father). She quickened the room with laughter in a way I did not recognize nor remember. With a pained heart I thought: *She's happy.* (Later, to comfort Father, Beybars would say: "That woman. An egma." He meant an enigma, and he was right.)

After breakfast Mother and I hit the hot streets. She was no longer at the Viennoise: "Spinsters and fussbudgets! They expected me asleep by ten!"; had spent one "horrible week" at the Anglo-German House: "A nightmare! They told me to take off my shoes, I couldn't smoke; God! *How they split hairs!*"; would have loved the Atholl (right next to the Fleurent and the Regent bars): "But I'd die before living in a place called the Atholl!" She had settled on the Minerva, "sweet" on Soliman Pasha. "Look!" She rushed me through a cluttered, sunny room papered green and gold to a balcony delirious with flowering jasmine. "All this!" Mother exulted, "and no sniveling doily fetishists!"

Ah! Mother's place! Everything she touched landed on the floor, and it was impossible to walk around without catching a foot in the strap of an apricot brassiere or kicking over a box of powder. The suit that had caused such a sensation at the Sporting Club lay in a heap. It was the maid's day off:

"I need," she explained, her laughter excessive, "someone to undo the damage. *Daily.*" This had always been true. But the real scandal of Mother's *exalted carelessness*—and I can find no better way to describe it—was elsewhere. In the bathroom I stumbled upon her scattered and bloodied underthings abandoned as thoughtlessly as a bird sheds its feathers. Her bedroom, too, was littered with bloodstained clothes and sheets and I stood for a time in the hallway between these two rooms, cowed by the staggering evidence of her femaleness, feeling somehow ashamed, somehow *dispossessed.* I remember how nearly a year before, when we had first come to Cairo, a number of maids had left cursing Mother and slamming doors.

And there was something else. Something that had taken place years before when I was child of six or seven, when we were living in New Hampshire in our house near the meadow and the woods. Very early one morning I found Mother sprawled on the kitchen floor, covered with dirt and sobbing. Her feet, her hands were so filthy they looked as though they had been charred by fire, and her beautiful hair was matted with twigs and leaves. Although I recognized her, I ran to Father, awakening him with my screams: "A stranger! A stranger!" wanting in this way to punish her.

I would not be quieted. Even when Mother had bathed and put on a clean dress, I would not allow her to touch me.

"I got lost, Lizoo," she entreated. "Lost in the woods. And I started to run. And I fell—just behind the house there, see?" She pointed to a place beyond our backyard where the lawn gave way to the woods. "I'm your momma," she smiled, surprising me by rubbing her nose against mine, "even when I've got a dirty face."

———

I joined Mother on the balcony. She had made us glasses of hot mint tea, a thing she did admirably. We sipped the burning tea and watched the street. Across from us, men, impeccable in their dove grey, their white clothes, sat at diminutive tables drinking coffee and smoking; every once in a while someone would leap to his feet and dance, singing brief scraps of song. A few were playing dominoes.

"I used to play dominoes with your father," she told me. "And Parcheesi. And checkers. Even bridge." A honking taxi captured our attention, and we looked on as two men attempted to coax a donkey from the center of the street. Mother said: "How I love Cairo's ill-tempered animals!"

A fantastic ambulant kitchen furnished with brass pans and trimmed with cut glass came into view. The covered pans held steaming food, and as I write this down I long for the Cairo of "Old Time"—that is to say "My Time"— the Cairo of the fifties when the air did not smell of car exhaust but of long-simmered lamb and fresh coffee, the comforting smell of animal dung and mint tea and jasmine.

"We tried craps," Mother said. "Gin rummy. Once I beat your father at Go."

A posture master materialized upon the sidewalk of the café; already he was performing. Mother and I nibbled dates and figs and sugar cookies, and watched him.

"Here we are," said Mother, "like the ladies of noble houses who once sat above the street monster gazing. Do you know why I love Cairo *so much*? It's because the public streets and coffee houses offer such *private* pleasure!" She laughed her deep laugh, her laugh of late nights and fresh limes and black honey; her scarlet, her glittering laugh. From the street a man looked up and, seeing her sitting above him in a bower of jasmine, smiled. When Mother returned his smile, his eyes flashed, and it seemed a powerful electric storm swept over us. Mother did not look away but instead raised an ironical eyebrow, an eyebrow that said: *Are you up for this? Are you up for a woman as blond as this? Can you afford her?*

Stunned, even troubled, he looked away. All this happened with such velocity only the heart could trace its passage. This revelation, the revelation of Mother's nature, gave way to confusion. Confusion knotted in my head like twine.

"Mother!" I exploded, scandalized. "You smiled at that stranger!"

"The curious thing about strangers, Liz," she murmured, "is that they need not be strangers for long." Looking down the street I saw that, in the gathering shadows of evening, the man lingered.

"No one!" I shouted, rising and stamping my foot, "behaves like this!" Perceptibly, the balcony shuddered and dipped.

Plunging her fingers deep in her hair, Mother said: "Stop grouching."

ELEVEN

Attar

Father had become strange yet claimed to be "better." "I ache from top to bottom," he grumbled to his mirror's reflection, and, as a "joke" when Beybars asked him how he was: "I'm stewing in my own juices!" Also, out of nowhere, and more than once, I heard him bark: *"Stop!"*

"Why do you keep saying that?" I asked, unable to contain myself. Father looked caught. Mortified.

"My head's in a pickle," he explained. "I'm telling it to stop. There's a passel of weasels in my brain, biting one another's tails. They're going round and round!" He grinned as though none of this mattered.

"A *passel*?"

"Well . . ." he reflected. "That's not quite right. Not a passel. A pride? No! Good God! That's lions!" He rapped his skull with his fist. "What *do* weasels come in?" He was off, nose in books for hours, swept away in accounts of wars beginning with the letter *P.*

Ramses Ragab came over that evening. The roses were blooming in Fayum, and we had not seen much of him. "How is your father?" he whispered when I met him at the door.

"He talks to himself," I said.

"What does he say?"

"He says: 'Stop!' and . . ." It was painful to continue.

"And?" With delicacy he stroked my wrist with his finger, a naked place between my two bracelets of red glass.

"He has nightmares."

"Such as?"

"Last night he dreamed he was in a very fast elevator *on his way to the stratosphere*. He was afraid that once he got there he would not be able to breathe and would die."

"It is a catastrophe to lose love," Ramses Ragab whispered. "But it is high time he mended." As always I was touched by the intimate light of his eyes. "The harvest has begun," he said, "and the distillation unremitting, night and day. I am returning to Fayum tomorrow. Let's get you both packed, and I'll come for you in the morning. You'll see the roses—well! There's no way *not* to see them! The divine roses of Damascus, Lizzie! We are making attar!" Intoxicated, I gazed into his eyes. Silently, I willed him to touch my wrist again. Instead he spoke: "And you'll see Sakkiet's village—she's there now; everyone is helping with the harvesting. And you'll see all my childhood haunts. You'll meet my mother and the housekeeper, Khadija; you'll be swept off your feet and so will *mon général*. At least I hope so! Ah! Here he is!"

"We're going to Fayum tomorrow!" I cried, running to put my arm around him. How slender he was! His fez seemed to rock on his bony head. "Ramses Ragab is taking us!" Father was silent. "You *must* say yes."

"And you must stop calling me 'Ramses Ragab,' " Ramses Ragab said. "Can't you call me 'Ram,' Lizzie? Like everybody else?"

"Everybody calls you *Ram*?" For some reason this suggestion put me out of temper. "Does Sakkiet call you *Ram*?"

"Sakkiet?" He looked bewildered. "No. But I'm her employer, and besides, the village has its customs. It would cause a scandal were she to call me Ram."

The next morning when we had left Cairo behind us, delighting in the false intimacy our window views provided and the equally false sense of "starting over," and as the land lay before us like an open hand, Father's eyes took on some sparkle.

"Quelle aventure!" he said.

———

Some memories have such heat that like stars and despite their age, their light continues to reach us. The first thing I remember about Fayum is the face of the girl Sakkiet, her eyes *wantoning* in the shadow of a bouquet of pink roses. She had pinned the roses to a gold cloth with which she had bound her hair. I was impressed by the novelty, the drama of her red-and-gold dress, the intoxication of her insolent face.

Sakkiet was frowning; anger appeared to covet her lovely mouth. I did not know she had been told to entertain me.

In Fayum there were roses, roses and water everywhere, and when the sun set, as it is setting now, behind the reedy shallows of the irrigation ditches, everything is ablaze and topsy-turvy—the sky the color of roses and the land a mirror of the sky. To my infinite surprise, Sakkiet has seized my hand and like lions we are swiftly and silently running to a grove of palm trees as in that bright air, everything dissolves: Cairo, my mother, even Father's *défaillance*—everything but the roses, the scent of roses, the roses tied to Sakkiet's hair, the palm grove nearly upon us, the voices of geese, the creaking of waterwheels and again, Sakkiet, "his" Sakkiet, running barefoot in a party dress and seeding the world with danger and delight. Delight because the scent of roses is marvelous; danger because Sakkiet, out of her laboratory duster and all in spangles, is *stunning* and, at fourteen, *marriageable.* Because I insist, and stubbornly, that there is a real risk Ramses Ragab loves her and is only waiting for her to grow into more of a woman. If I were a man, I would love her: her provoking face, her deeply lashed and lacquered eyes, her insolence, her bright butterfly ways. You see: thirteen was for me an idolatrous age.

Yet I am so grateful she has seized my hand, so stunned all the gods of Egypt are housed in my heart and the sky arches over us with grace. In this world of water and roses, love spills from one person to the next; like fragrance, like water, its quality is restlessness.

Then, just as suddenly as we had set off running, we are sitting side by side in the staggered shadow of the palm grove, and Sakkiet is sucking a thorn from her big toe and looking at me with a mind-boggling mix of restless curiosity, jealousy, and contempt. (If I were a painter, I would paint Sakkiet exactly like this: her eyes raised to mine, her lips pressed to her toe, her knee in the air, her dress rioting around her.) When I offer her a shy smile, it is received with a grunt. *"Assif,"* I sputter, thrashing about for something to say. *I'm sorry*—an apology for not speaking Arabic, but Sakkiet—because she was coralled into this outing—misunderstands. She shrugs and spits a splinter in my general direction but not *at* me—a victory of sorts—and continues to nibble away at my softer parts with her eyes.

"Look!" I try next, lifting my wrist into the sunlight so that the glass bangles sparkle, *"Jolie, non? Gameel?"* I want her to acknowledge that I, too, satisfy Beauty's exactions. Besides—I am tired of worshiping her. When she touches the bangles with interest, I toss my head—a gesture borrowed from Mother. With erotic ease Sakkiet kneels and, unpinning the roses from her hair, pulls the cloth free. And then she is taking my hair in her hands and binding it, see: already she has pinned the roses above my ear. Their petals touch my cheek. Now Sakkiet waits for the gift I have unknowingly promised her. I slip the bracelets off my wrist with sudden sorrow, but when Sakkiet receives them, leaning to me, kissing me swiftly, my heart surges. Her kiss is the cipher that contains all the powers of the day: Fayum, its waters, its roses, Ramses Ragab. *Ram.* I must remember to name him differently.

With a shimmer, shouting *Yalla!*, Sakkiet seizes my hand again and before I can scramble to my feet she is already tugging me up and away. I touch the roses, afraid they will become undone, but they hold. The fabric with which she has bound my hair is studded with small blue stars.

Roses give way to fields of henna and these in turn to gardens of coriander. All the edges of Fayum are marked by gardens: of cucumbers, onions, melons . . . *Iwa!* the soft edges of Fayum! We are close by the village now and a small boy standing in a patch of beans raises his mulberry staff in greeting, a girl shouts Sakkiet's name; already in the near distance the great marshy lake shimmers with birds. There's a new smell in the air, invigorating and medicinal.

"Bartoo' aan!" Sakkiet breathes deeply as she runs. Squinting I see bitter oranges. *Bartoo' aan:* a bright and bitter name containing all the convulsive beauty of things.

Later, when I would learn that it was Ramses Ragab who told Sakkiet to bring me here—"Let her soul," he had said, "be flooded with beauty"—I also learned that the palm grove—at no great distance from the house—was visible from his laboratory window and that he had seen us. "It touched my heart," he told me, with a gesture of his long fingers, "to see two raven-haired beauties taking their ease in the light and the shadow of the trees. And what," he had asked, "do you think of Fayum?" To convey my pleasure, I had spread out my arms and spun about the room. "I see," he said when I stopped, "Sakkiet gave you her roses."

"It was a trade. I gave her my bracelets." I held out my bare arm.

"Here in Fayum," he teased me, "that is an unfair exchange. Sakkiet, as is her habit, has gotten the better deal!" I wondered at this. "It's my fault," he continued, "if Sakkiet is somewhat . . . spoiled. Yes—at times I fear I've spoiled her but her future is so grim! As long as she prefers to run around without shoes I like to think her soul is safe, although she has enough party dresses to satisfy the dowry requirements of twelve fussy grooms." All at once he looked sad. "She's a free spirit, our Sakkiet," he said softly. "At least she's a free spirit *for now.*"

"But why can't she always be that way?" I was envious of his acute interest in her.

"They will marry her." He said this bitterly. "Sometime soon." He added, "Her position here is unique. Because of the work she does for me she is something of a celebrity. She's expensive, in other words. For now this protects her. Her rarity, but also her wild ways! I will hate," he said then, "to see my Sakkiet veiled. I have offered to educate her; I have tried to convince her family that she could live an extraordinary life. But the extraordinary terrifies them. I have tried," he said miserably, "to shake up the old ways for so long now!" He gazed out the window to a place in the sky where doves were wheeling. "If only there was a way to keep the beauty of Old Time safe, but not its *tragic foolishness!*"

Memories accumulate within the mind like the disparate fragrances that make a perfume. Our only means of recovering the past and yet how volatile they are! In my private *Rosarium Philosophorum,* the memory book of my own origins and sympathies, the Fayum surges more as a process of alchemy than a place: the stench of mud dissolving into the sublime fragrance of roses. The roses themselves distilled into something far subtler: attar.

Earlier I mentioned Ramses Ragab's laboratory window with its view of the palm grove. Beneath it he had set a small fan-shaped table. It was here with only a limited palette of scents that he devoted himself to the subtle process of recovery, the revery that enabled him to return to the past, to imagine a world spelled by blue lotus and white ibis, a world in which each fossil shell was a gift from the moon, and each willow, each sycamore, each drop of rain divine. A world entirely free of the stench of burning rubber, the bitter fumes of coal, of car exhaust and even *vulgar plastics in decomposition*! (He insisted he could smell the stench of decomposing celluloid dice—"a little like rancid butter and the droppings of swallows"—and had given Father a new set of ivory.)

At that time Ramses Ragab was wanting to uncover the secret of *setj-heb*—a feast day perfume that contained styrax and benzoin. He told us, Father and me, that his *olfactory reveries* depended upon subtle evocations of the past that included ancient myths, hymns, and erotic poetry. When he was in Cairo, he spent a good amount of time each week in the museum, and when in Fayum, reflecting for hours in nature, "nose to the breeze."

"There is an ancient text," he told us, "that was written down and preserved in Thebes. It is a hymn to the Nile. It evokes the black earth of the river's conception, the silt that causes the greening of the world; it praises the Nile for loving kindness and exhaustively describes the seasonal flowering of plants, the flourishing of antelope and oxen and geese, the sacrifice of the fat calf in acknowledgment of this munificence.

"My life has been devoted to the task of illuminating, by way of perfume, the beautiful obscurity of the past. Always I am after a scent worthy of this ancient sensibility that will evoke a loving kindness in the heart of those who wear it. It is like . . . what is it like?" he thought for a moment. "Like melting down the bright wax of the world's hum and buzz into one perfect grain of intense delight. An *atom*," he demonstrated with his fingers, "of delight." His excitement, his pleasure in the life he had chosen for himself was thrilling. "I've told you—I must have! That it takes two hundred and fifty pounds of petals to make an ounce of attar?" As so often when near him, I was flooded with heat. I could not imagine an older woman feeling greater heat for a man than I did at that instant.

"There is a lovely poem in Old Egyptian that may have sounded something like this—" Eyes closed, he recited a poem that might have been a song or a prayer. Then, in English:

> Her chamber is open to you,
> yet she pretends to sleep.
> The door hangings caress your face
> and her scent knows your name.
> Then . . . the muffled sound of her laughter!

Writing this, other memories propose themselves, but I do not know where to put them! So I will list them, list them like the ingredients of a perfume, a perfume named "The Fayum."

—I recall ducks in the reedy shallows of a ditch, and sheldrakes, and even storks. A one-eyed pelican, abandoned and alone, caused me to sob in Father's arms.

—A child who held a palm branch over Sakkiet and me and chased away the flies as we sat beside the lake.

—Again: Sakkiet. The skin of her face, the whites of her eyes, the light ringing in her hair: *pearls*. All pearls! (And not the domestic kind, either.)

—The dates were ripening in clusters. Still green, they cascaded from the crowns of the trees like fountains.

—In the village: a camel painted on a blue door. On another door, a ship.

—Father in sandals—a prodigy. And despite doctor's orders, very busy with a pipe that had belonged to Ramses Ragab's father and which his mother insisted he smoke "with impunity and even impudently" as she looked for an unopened tin of tobacco and found it, squirreled away in a cabinet containing a weird collection of porcelain incense burners in the shape of tree trunks, and a peculiar lamp that was meant to perfume the air with "Hungary water."

—Walking with Ramses Ragab, Father and I, and talking about Old Time again. This was at dawn and the roses were being harvested before the heat of the sun could destroy their scent. The gardens were full of people and all in a festive mood. Shouting, laughter, the music of flutes.

Father became stuck on a fantasy he called "Pharaohs of the Future" in which tycoons, "having bled dry the self-deluded fellaheen of Capital," paid "Last-Rattle technocrats to have their corpses kept in refrigerated sarcophagi, their valuables safe at their feet in canopic jars, their holdings watched by notaries trained in the Second Coming and its vagaries." The entire enterprise would be administered by "madmen and their hirelings: laboratory technicians, cleaning staff, night watchmen, not to forget the suave pickpockets and racketeers in public relations!

"Imagine," said Father, growing more and more agitated, "great chilled pyramids of blue glass shadowing Wall Street and studded with the bodies of the rich, napping as they wend their way—or so they thought when signing the agreement—to a new existence, restored to youth by inventions—hopefully only temporarily virtual—as the rest of us, condemned to mortality and its cruel inevitabilities, trod the dusty, dung-laden street below like peasants."

"As are all dandies, you are a cynic!" Ramses Ragab laughed, putting his arm around Father and giving him a friendly squeeze. Father had developed a slight nervous twitch that he did his best to conceal by the manipulation of his borrowed pipe, tobacco, and lighter.

This fantasy of Father's, by the way, has me reflecting on the curious contradictions that riddled his character. It was so like him, so very like him, to complain about tycoons and the plight of the common man, and in the next breath extol the merits of monarchies—"not 'corrupt' monarchies, mind you (such as Farouk's)"—but he had a soft spot for the Prince of Monaco (whom he resembled) and the thought of that "pristine and minuscule principality" caused his eyes to mist over.

"I hope you don't think my garden world is anything like that 'pristine principality,' " Ramses Ragab said. (Pristine principality! I inwardly groaned. Father continued to be greatly taken with the letter *P*.) "The gardens are an experiment," Ramses Ragab continued, "some say an experiment in socialism. I prefer to say in humanity. I would have it no other way, although to tell the truth the idea is not mine but my mother's, whose hatred of feudalism is visceral. Father, on the other hand, was of the old school," he added. "Our experiment is only a few decades young.

"The villagers call the gardens and their network of ditches 'our chain of miracles' and, indeed, the village and its people are flourishing. The *Kosmèterion,* the production of attar, of absolute of henna and tuberose—these enable us *all* to live well. Mother and I are only two among the many the land provides for. We are fortunate that the villagers delight in beauty as much as we do, and believe that to devote a life to beauty is honorable." He looked at Father who, catching his breath, was gazing out at the rose gardens and the many people toiling in the pale light.

"A moral being cannot see himself as 'above' another," Ramses Ragab said. "This is why monarchy is execrable. Surely you see that?"

"Yet some people are more gifted, more intelligent—" Father muttered somewhat evasively. He was looking at the workers in the fields as though in their redundant clothes of blue and white and black—and despite the fact that they waved and called out greetings—they were of another species.

"Aren't intelligence, beauty, and the other gifts of chance their own rewards? What I mean to say," Ramses Ragab spoke with great earnestness, "is: to be born beautiful or intelligent is not a badge of honor!" Father gazed at his friend, visibly startled. "Nor is it a *fault!* Such gifts need to be accepted by the lucky individual with humility and, I think, embraced by the community as good fortune. In this small corner of the Fayum, I expect intelligence to be honored, although it is true that here as elsewhere unique capacities do create resentment and even distrust. Fathers are especially terrified of a thoughtful daughter. Daughters are cursed by the most persistent, the most nefarious of inequalities." He turned to me. "It is not because they live in Paradise that the villagers dare allow themselves to be generous when it comes to their own women. I imagined," he went on as the lake and its birds came to meet us, "I *still* imagine that this place has all the chances of becoming one of exemplary life. But, you know—for utopia to become a reality, each individual must have the courage to harbor utopia within."

The lake was empty of boats, and as the sun was rising, trembled with light.

"No one is fishing today but the birds," Ramses Ragab laughed. "Every single person is out gathering flowers. We shall have to eat roast duck for lunch. I hope you don't mind?"

—Each evening before dinner the old housekeeper, Khadija, drew me a bath and, as I tested it with my foot, scattered the water with orange peel, saying: *Peace be with you!* (And each morning at breakfast an enormous pot of orange marmalade was set out on the table!)

As I soaked my body in that cozy and mysterious room, the tiles collected dew, the mirror steamed over, and the voices and clatter from the kitchen reached me through a haze. In this house *pleasure* pulled the strings of sympathy!

—What else? My sheets smelled of sunlight, my room of potpourri. ("A good potpourri lasts fifty years," Ramses Ragab's mother proudly told me; "the ones in all the rooms were made ten years ago. Rose petals," she began in answer to my question, "and jasmine, allspice, and cloves. You're a sweet child." Her interest in me ended there.)

—There was a cabinet piled with books that tempted me each time I entered my room. For the most part bound in paper and cut by hand, they smelled of pipe tobacco and vetiver—Ramses Ragab's father had been a tireless reader. One of these I recall with real affection. It, too, smelled like its owner. It was the classic work by Theophrastus: *On Odours,* and the old man had flooded the margins with notes. This book fascinated me especially because I knew it must be one of the books Ramses Ragab had read as a boy. Perhaps it was the book that awakened his initial, his searching interest in perfume.

On Odours proposed any number of mysteries, for example the phrase: *Indeed some animals seem to be annoyed by odours, even good ones, if what is said of vultures and beetles be true; the explanation is that their natural character is antipathetic to odours.* What, I wondered, is said of vultures and beetles? And by whom?

In the marvelous intimacy of Mr. Ragab's room, I decided to investigate. In a crumbling illustrated edition of Buffon I found the scarab at once, the scarab that *lives in the excrement of animals.* Turning the page I found another beetle that *smells strongly of tobacco* and then another that lives, *as vultures do,* on rotting corpses. *Vultures,* the book continued, *may be recognized by their scent.* I wondered: just how trustworthy was this Theophrastus, anyway? And I found a beetle, a "musk" beetle that smells not of musk at all, but of: *attar!*

"Science," Ramses Ragab explained over grilled bread

and marmalade, "was riddled with confusion until very recently. Theophrastus did not always proceed rigorously, depending instead on superstition and the idle gossip of perfume sellers. Nonetheless, his book is full of treasures, Lizzie. Don't abandon him too quickly!"

I summoned up the courage to ask his mother if I might borrow it, passing it to her across the breakfast table. She took it from me, put it to her nose, breathed in deeply, smiled, nodded, and handed it over with the words:

"See to it that you bring it back with its fragrance intact." (Ramses Ragab's mother, regal in a perpetual crown of silver braids (and this despite her politics) smelled of Jicky: "the *only* perfume."

—I recall how the tiled floors of my room smelled of brown soap; the entire house was haunted by the faintest ghost of mildew, and smoke—old and new—from the kitchen fire. Henna leaves hung drying from the attic rafters, and these, too, gave the house its own particular fragrance. How I loved the house in Fayum, its soft edges, the purity of its whitewashed walls, the reassuring permanence of its deep thresholds and green tiled floors, the thoughtful impermanence of its perfumes. I felt safe there, as I had not felt safe for a long time, perhaps never, and this realization caused me to turn my kerosene lamp's bright brass key, and plunged into darkness, my face pressed to my pillow, to cry alone and gratefully each night. How tiresome it was that Mother had left, how thin the atmosphere of our house in Cairo!

But here. Here every nook and cranny radiated quiet and the warmth of the years. Even the furniture—all of it— seemed to be daydreaming.

(Not very long ago, while on a visit to Hermopolis, I came upon this text, inscribed upon a temple wall:

> He has planted an excellent garden
> All around his house.
> Each flower, each flowering tree
> Blesses this house.)

———

An important memory is like a gravitational field—the mind is compelled to return to it again and again. It is like a moon; it lives in light and shadow.

Before we all returned to Cairo, Sakkiet and I took another walk. I bound my hair in the starred scarf *in her manner* and pinned a single rose above my ear—I could not manage more. But she looked pleased when she saw what I had done and, touching the scarf she had given me, cried *da minee*! My gift to you. Then she jingled the glass bracelets in my face and laughed.

It was late in the day and the gardens were empty of people. However, as we took the path to the lake, a fellah approached us carrying a hoe. When she saw him, Sakkiet took my hand and held it tightly. He was walking quickly and soon stood directly in front of us. He did not greet us, but only raised his arm to wipe the sweat from his face. Then with a terrible and unexpected urgency, he began to scold Sakkiet. I touched the scarf and its stars as if for protection, and holding my breath toyed with the rose above my ear. All around us the lovely soft edges of things were tearing.

When his voice became shrill and threatening, Sakkiet turned her face away in an attempt to isolate herself. In this way she had hid her face from him; in this way she had somehow ceased to be. She still held my hand. And murmured something so dark and low he did not hear her but kept on ranting. Pulling me close, her lashes thick with tears, Sakkiet pushed past him. Together we moved away down the narrow path, although he was shouting. In the next instant he had picked up some dung from the path.

When the dung slammed into the back of her head, Sakkiet froze. She looked like a replica of herself, stained and cracked. I thought: *He will kill her with his hoe,* and the skin of my back flattened like a dog's. Instead he cleared his throat and spat. Sakkiet and I stood together without moving for what seemed a very long time. When we broke apart at last and looked around us, we were alone. But I knew the drama of which Ramses Ragab had spoken was upon her. Shuddering, I held her; we held each other.

All around us: the din of waterwheels and geese.

Father and I returned to Cairo the next day with Ramses Ragab and bundles of petals, gathered that morning, to be prepared in maceration in the laboratory of the *Kos-*

mètèrion; the fact that small quantities of essence were produced in the ancient manner on the premises was one of the *Kosmètèrion's* principal charms.

"Your mother," Ramses Ragab said to me as we approached Cairo (and Father was softly snoring in the backseat), "will want some of the fresh essence prepared with almond oil. She says it is the secret of her beauty. I tell her, with humility, that the secret of her beauty is Fate." How I hated to hear him speak of Mother's beauty! "She bought a little gift for you the last time she came. Did it please you?"

"I haven't opened it yet," I said.

"Open it," he told me. "I am the one who chose it for you."

"What do you think of my mother?" I whispered, suddenly irresistibly curious. Father continued to snore, delicately, like a bubbling water pipe.

Ramses Ragab said:

"There are women like lionesses. It is their nature to prowl. She is like this. And this is her mystery, Lizzie; her mystery and her tragedy, perhaps. Well . . ." he smiled, turning to face me briefly, "I like her *famishment,* you know? It is about life. So, to answer your question, I think of her this way: a famished lioness, on the prowl. There are others like her in Cairo. Women and men both. I am telling you this," he turned to me again, "because I know I'm not telling you anything new."

"But why?" I asked, angrily. "Why is she famished?"

"She came from a cold country," he said. "Perhaps she carries a piece of ice with her wherever she goes. Perhaps she hopes to melt that ice in Cairo. Perhaps this is why she haunts the *Kosmètèrion,* asking for my 'hottest' perfumes. Perhaps she thinks that if she radiates heat long enough she will be transformed from lioness to woman—" Then, without warning, he recited:

Anoint yourself, my beloved,
and your flesh, your bones
the marrow of your bones
your heart and all your vital organs
will be blessed
your body will quiver and quicken
will take on the heat of the sun
the heat of the world
the heat of the living
the heat, O my sister,
of lovers, coupling . . .

TWELVE

Sleeping with Schéhérazade

The night of our return from Fayum, Father's and mine, I took Theophrastus to bed with me. From my bedroom window I could see the neighbor's roof illuminated by a full moon, and a lonely sheep awaiting sacrifice. Pigeons were raised on that roof also, pigeons Beybars bartered for and prepared so lovingly. And there was an admirable tomato plant the size of a small tree, its fruit as sweet as plums. For a time I sat gazing out the window holding the book to my face, testing its fragrance. The Fayum surged in memory: my room and its lamp, the green lake and its birds, the still gardens sustained by their gridworks of bright water, the gardeners and harvesters themselves reduced by distance to ciphers as they are painted on the walls of tombs. I opened the book and read:

> Moisture belongs to plants . . . this moisture is
> attended by a taste . . . all plants have most mois-

ture at the time of making growth. Again, in some plants the juice has a special color; in some it is white, as in those which have a milky juice; in some blood-red, as in centaury—

These words acted upon me like a sequence of charms and as I continued to read, I felt the presence of Ramses Ragab distinctly, as I had throughout that entire week even when he had vanished into his laboratory to dream at his little fan-shaped table.

Again in some plants the juice is merely thick, as in those in which it is of milky character . . . the juice of the silphium is pungent like the plant itself.

Reading Theophrastus was an operation of grace, of grace and deep magic—as when I read my beloved *Arabian Nights* and the perceptible world dissolved:

I have known love and passion since infancy; I was nourished at my mother's breasts—

Words that spelled the night with urgency, a kind of stunning clarity:

—In all plants mentioned the juice either forms naturally—

Something like an undiluted sublimity:

—or when the incisions are made. But it is obvious
that men only make incisions in plants whose juice
is sought after such as myrrh which should be cut
at the rising of the dog star and on the hottest
days—

Thinking: *on the hottest days.* Thinking: *moisture is
attended by a taste.* Thinking: *My longing is violent; it sub-
merges me in heat. None like it existeth.* Reading Theophrastus: *They first pound it up in sweet wine.* Recalling these
words of Schéhérazade: and *O how sweet are the nights.*

It is dark, Schéhérazade recited, it is dark and my
transport and my disease are excited, and desire
provoketh my pain.

Imagining what it would be, what it must be to be
naked in the naked arms of a man; what it might be to be
incised, penetrated by a man. *And the root is stout and sweet,*
wrote Theophrastus. *The fruit is good for the eye.*

Imagining for the first time, fearlessly, the reality of a
girl *being sexual* (a term of my mother's) with a man. I
thought of Sakkiet, wondering what it would be to be
betrothed against one's will. Imagining, in a sudden fever,
what it would be to be betrothed to Ramses Ragab against
my will. These are the thoughts that thrust me into plea-

sure's heady orbit, pleasure, like an act of magic, flooding the hours of the night with fragrancy.

For Schéhérazade, love was like a game of chess played in bed upon the counterpane, its moves could not be counted. Schéhérazade enchanted the king Schahriar not only with her stories within stories, but her moves within moves.

It is dark and desire—

When I closed my eyes, everything vanished and all that was left was this: My resurgent secret, exotic and irresistible, that "sweet tradition of little girls" Saleh once laughingly said; all that was left was pleasure, and its attainment the only operation of sympathy that mattered. My pleasure wantoning like a wilderness in his mutable embrace, gazing into his many faces, alone in the middle of the night, having returned home from Fayum on the hottest of days, in the season of roses, in the season of the making of attar.

And the beauty of delight hath appeared with perfume.

———

When I awoke, the moon had abandoned my window, and both books—*On Odours* and *The Arabian Nights*—were sprawled beside me. I lay in the luxury and silence of solitude and thought about Schéhérazade, her beauty and intelligence. The first time she sleeps with Schahriar, she offers to recite *a moral tale disguised as a licentious one,* saying that, unlike lesser mortals, he will appreciate the difference. She has just lost her virginity to Schahriar, and in a few hours her neck will be broken. In order to survive she needs to inebriate the king's soul. The prophet tells men to cultivate their wives as one cultivates a garden: this is just what Schéhérazade does to Schahriar. Night after night she cultivates him in the infinite revery that glimmers at the heart of human sexuality. Night after night she provokes the king's curiosity and his desire, just as she softens his lethal rage against women and reveals the feminine sympathies that animate the world: the rose, the shell, the female sex; the female face, the moon; her saliva and the nectar of flowers, the taste of grapes having ripened on the vine. She reveals the *sympathy* between sensual love and adventure; she reveals that love is both the reason for adventure and its reward. Love, Schéhérazade tells Schahriar, is the Universe's soul—indissoluble and indestructible. Without love's ardor to animate it, the Universe would be as lifeless as a handful of sand. Everything is perceived through the senses, she reminds him; it is the imagining mind that makes the world intelligible, and nothing animates the imagination as does love. It is love that makes us human, spontaneous, and thoughtful; it is the highest bond and the greatest good. The world and all its forms belong to Eros, and when everything is ended love will persist. Ardor, Schéhérazade tells Schahriar, is the world's cause and the world's reason. When Schéhérazade speaks, it is as if the words themselves are wantoning.

At the end of the book, the storyteller is a queen and her sister, Dinarzade, has become a woman. She, too, sleeps with Schahriar. Dinarzade has never left her sister's side; she has listened to all her stories and witnessed their lovemaking. I imagined that Sakkiet and I were sisters, that Ramses Ragab was Schahriar and that we shared his embraces. Flowers were threaded in our hair, and our hands and feet were stained with henna. We smelled of Susinum. He desired us above all others, but between the two of us he could not decide. His counterpane heaved with our laughter.

In *The Arabian Nights,* the descriptions of what a desirable woman is are repeated again and again like a conjuration. Perfect beauty united:

The voluptuousness of the Greeks, the amorous virtues of the Egyptians, the lascivious movements of the women of Arabia, the heat of the daughters of the Ethiopians, the limitless knowledge of India's temple whores, the unbridled passions of the women of Nubia, the narrow cunts of the daughters of the Chinese, the vigor of the women of Irak, the delicacy and knowledge of perfumes of the Persians, the muscular thighs of the women of Upper Egypt . . .

and so on. That night I wrote a letter to Ramses Ragab. And because I could not bring myself to write "Ram" or even "Ramses," and because I knew it would be ludicrous to write a love letter and use his full name, I decided simply to begin:

It is very late and the Moon which was full and bright over the neighbor's roof is gone and I am alone, no, I am not alone because my heart is full of the fragrances of Fayum, your mother's Jicky and your father's books and always the smell of roses and the knowledge that you were near.

I know you think I am a child but I am only one year younger than Sakkiet, who will be married soon.
And I want
and I wish that
I wish

I was unable to go further. I could not name what it was I wished for, what it was I wanted. I could not, I dared not write: *I want you to make love to me.* I could not, I dared not write: *I want you to take me.* But then, suddenly seized by my own boundless longing, I began to write quickly, as though I was about to die and needed at all cost to write everything down; as though I would die like a fish out of water if I didn't write everything down at once:

I am dreaming of our naked bodies pressed together in a garden of roses, a garden of lilies, in a garden of henna, in the bed Schéhérazade shared with Schahriar. You once told me that I smelled of new pencils and grapefruit and green sandalwood, but I smell only of sandalwood and rose attar—the fragrance you gave me; it is a woman's fragrance. And it says in my copy of The Arabian Nights *that dark girls have a* hidden sensibility, *and I think this is so because I always know as soon as you enter our house what fragrances you have been making. Like the seasons of the air your perfume changes from one day to the next; sometimes it seems from one moment to the next, as though being near you was like being in a garden where many flowers grow and their perfume is carried on the breeze; sometimes it is jasmine that scents the air; sometimes it is the flowering quinces. Or a man is passing in the street selling cinnamon and everything changes, the mood of the day changes entirely. He is selling fried dough dipped in honey; he is offering freshly roasted coffee in cups perfumed with mastic; he is roasting almonds; he is turning lamb on the spit; he is boiling the mint for tea.*

I cannot place or name you. You are too "volatile"—a word you taught me. I think you are mysterious.

In my book (I'm still talking about The Arabian Nights*) it says young girls smell like nard and that this has a wonderful smell. I wonder if this is true, and if you were lying beside me breathing my skin,*

*would you say, "Lizzie, you smell like nard." It also
says that it is best for a man to be with a girl and I
think this must be so. But if you think I am still too
young, we could wait for a year because then I'll be
fourteen, the age Sakkiet is now, and there will be no
reason not to love me then if you love me now. I hope
you will read my letter and tell me if you love me;
sometimes I think you do. I think you love me when I
look up and see you are gazing at me and your eyes
warm me as though suddenly the air in the room came
directly from Fayum, Fayum under the midday sun
when everything is still—even the birds—and everyone is resting in the shade. At noon when the scent of
roses is so strong everyone is dizzy.*

*I have read that nard is found in the Himalaya
Mountains and that it grows at seventeen thousand
feet! So it is very rare. And I have read that in the
Tamil language "nard" is the word for everything that
smells good. Once you gave me some to smell; you put
a drop on my wrist. It was strange but wonderful, a
little like valerian and patchouly at the same time.
Green and gold, cold and hot! I wish . . .*

*I want to go to you now, this instant, and ask you
to put your nose to my wrist and tell me if I smell of a
schoolgirl's pencils, or if I smell of* nard!

*People think that in order to harvest mandrake
you have to whisper to the plant about the mysteries of
love. And this is because the root of the mandrake is*

*just like a human person: it is female or it is male. I
think my letter to you is like a mandrake harvest
because I am telling you my deepest mystery. Please
read my letter and answer it as soon as you can because
I am like a plant that needs water, I am like a mandrake that has heard all about love and wants to be
pulled. I think I am dying for you. Yes. This is what is
happening. I am dying for you.*

    Lizzie

After I wrote this letter I pressed the cipher I had tat-
tooed to my wrist with a pin so that it pained me and bled
a little, and this to ease my longing, the pain in my heart. A
drop of blood pearled at the center of the cipher; it tasted
sweet. I thought to needle the cipher was to *needle him,* if
only a little. I took up my letter and read it.

My letter was impossible! It was ridiculous—the letter
of a precocious schoolgirl. If he read it, he would laugh in
that quiet way he had; he would laugh indulgently; he
would indulge me and be kind, nothing more. He was a
man of the world—hadn't Mother once told me so? *A man
of the world, even if he comes across so damned precious, you
know?* I supposed it was true; clearly it was true. He was a
man of the world who had dealings every day with the
most beautiful, the most sophisticated women of Cairo,
women whom I now imagined as versions of Mother, big-
bodied, full-bosomed women with coltish legs and *wantoning* eyes who, as they received their precious purchase from

his own hand—the coveted jar of cream, the unique perfume—would whisper a name and a number and an hour.
They would meet, not in a field of flowers like some ridiculous Egyptian movie with someone wailing: *Habibi!*
Habibi! in the background over and over again, no, but
instead in a beautiful room tiled with blue stars in an
impasse planted with ancient trees, a room that their husbands knew nothing about, yes: these were handsome, cyn-
ical women, divorced or married to men too busy to notice
their wives vanished for hours altogether in the afternoon;
foreign women, Swedish tourists, for example, unmarried
and worldly, mad for Egyptian men; women unafraid to
write: I want to be penetrated by you; please meet me (but
no, they wouldn't plead!), *meet me,* rue Mouizz Lidin Illah,
Number 5, tomorrow, the blue door behind the fountain,
so that we may *pleasure each other* (a great phrase I'd also
picked up from *The Arabian Nights*); women, in other
words like Mother, who littered the floor with apricot
underwear and fucked even when bleeding. Again, self-
loathing welled up inside me: how I hated my body, just
barely female, my breasts like those green plums so small
one can hold half a dozen in the palm of the hand! Unlike
Mother's breasts, so damned gorgeous, her long legs—
would I ever grow tall? Mother, asleep on the other side of
the river, in the arms of strangers she eyed from her balcony, in her room filled with flowers rotting in their vases.
When she was awake, she was the embodiment of air, and
this is why I felt oppressed and had to fight to breathe.

Asleep she was the cipher for clay; I could imagine how heavy she would seem asleep beside her lover, all her quickness stilled, her breath smelling of the day's cigarettes, her body like a bank of sand soaking up the night, soaking up the radiant heat of another's body. I could not imagine her lying in my father's arms, only with a stranger, dark and lean, as bright as a dagger; a stranger like the one I'd seen her pressed to the afternoon Father and I returned from the Mouski and opened the door and the chess set of ivory tumbled to the floor and our lives began to fall and were still falling.

Sobbing now, I tore up my letter to Ramses Ragab, the man beyond reach, the older man, the worldly man, the gazelle man who came to our house almost every day *but not to see me,* not because he, too, longed to *pleasure me,* but because he shared—if to a lesser degree—Father's folly; the man who stretched out like an overgrown boy, having kicked off his impeccable, *man of the world* shoes; having dropped his linen jacket over a chair with a nonchalance that pierced me to the quick, to stretch out with a sigh on the Shiraz saying: *"Eh, bien! Mon général! On commence?"*

Popov Resurges

The Ottoman calligraphers created mazes of embellishments in which the text was secreted. Like a reflecting pool within a garden, the uncovered text is a revelation.

In the Egypt of Old Time, ☥, the sign for life, represented a mirror of copper, bright with stolen light. ☥ also represented the lace of a sandal as seen from above. To be alive is to be prepared to see and to walk.

———

Enlivened by the trip to Fayum, Father wished to walk, to explore our own little corner of Cairo. In those days, Gezira had many marvelous public gardens: the Pharaonic, for example. The Moorish and the Fish. The animal necropolis. Walking proved a fine antidote to Father's lingering bouts of melancholy and my own erotic languor.

With each passing day Father became more like his old self. His conversation, always somewhat mannered, was playful, even inspired. When, on a late afternoon, we visited the graves of dead house pets and horses, Father wondered aloud if these suggested frivolity, sadness, or delirium. Spying a dachshund's mausoleum, he decided on *pathological.* The dachshund had a stunning resemblance to *raw dough,* and its nearest neighbors—a doleful Scottie and a parrot—to *anchovy butter.* Father mused:

"Are *all* places of nostalgia in bad taste? Ah! But look! There's Popov!" So it was. Flanked by miniature obelisks, Popov bounced toward us in yellow sneakers, kicking up a cloud of sand and dust.

"Halloo! Halloo!" Popov called out, his arm extended as though a large dog were pulling him along on a leash. "Khow iz life? Khow iz life?" He pivoted with the grace of a hippopotamus in a pool and pointed to a porous house cat coiled like a turd on top of a sphere of veined marble. "Pretty cutsi, *da?*"

"Candle wax," said Father. "Pomade." Popov asked:

"Howzo?"

"We're imagining what the sculptures are made of," I explained.

"Oh! Ah! I *zee!*" Popov nodded, although clearly perplexed. He smelled of old clothes, cheap lavender cologne, and bad teeth. His fingers were smeared with ink, and I recalled that this was the very thing that had endeared him to Father when they first met. Inky fingers and the curious conviction that one day people would no longer be interested in reading novels, but instead books having to do with war, statistics, and game theory. We had not spent time with Popov since the day of our picnic when he had found the mummified finger.

"I cannotell you!" Popov bobbed up and down, "khow pleazing I am to havcompany!"

Twilight was nearly upon us, and the necropolis seemed stranger by the minute. We came upon a series of recent birds' graves all studded with pots of flowers. As the three of us took in a dun-colored raven, Popov recalled a recent epidemic.

"Tallow," Father said. "Saddlesoap."

"Oh! Ah! Izee!" Popov clapped his hands. "Datvon, *alabastar.*"

"It's about what they *look* like," I explained. "Not what they *are.*"

"Zey are notvery nice," Popov agreed. "If vuoz me, I vill be vuanting petsi *stuffed,* you zee? Lively-like. Glass eyeball. Nice tongue made ov rred ledderr or vuot hav we? *Papier-mâché.* Oh! Better! Japan lacquer! Now I'm talking. Lively, *in furr.* Da real petsi! Zstuffed. Under glass bell. Like—"

"Cheese." said Father.

"*Niet!* In wax-vuorking. I give an example."

"Not in this climate!"

"Ah! Oh! *True!*" We walked on. "Bird," Popov decided after reflection, "notgood petsi! But *zay!*" He leapt as if on springs, his hands clasping and unclasping. "Hav you *heard*?" (It astonishes me, even now, how the insignificant Popov managed within the next few moments to precipitate a crisis.)

"Heard?" Father supposed his colleague had news from the university.

"Da latezt bite of juizy—" Popov began launching, as he bounded about, a brief series of antipathies. "Da latezt bite ov gozzip?"

"It is late," Father said, uneasy. "Soon it will be evening. Another time. Another time . . ." He drifted off. It was always hard for Father who was, as he described himself, "*au fond* amiable," to hurt people's feelings. However, fear was upon him and, his arm in mine, he began to scurry toward the street.

"Ah! Ah! But anodder time, anodder time *too late*. Ve zay in Roossiya: gozzip roazt gooze. Better hot! Who vant goose cold? You tell me! *Naowboddy!*" He said this with vehemence.

"My daughter," Father put his arm around me protectively, "and I must get into town." He looked at his watch. "We have an invitation to dinner."

"Dinner? Iz tea time!"

"It is our custom," Father, growing irritable, said testily, "to eat lightly and go to bed early."

"Oh . . . Oh! It iz you fear gooze too hot forr girli!"

"Yes!" Father agreed. But what perverse instinct had me pull away from Father's arm and say with irritation:

"I'm not a *baby*! I wish everybody would—"

"Haou vold?"

"Thirteen."

"Zirrteen!" Popov clapped his hands. "Ha! In Roossiya vould be drinking wodka! Zewing daouwry!" As Popov spoke, Father gazed at me miserably and I flashed a guilty smile. Too late. I had given Popov permission to tell his story; already he had taken Father's arm.

"Vwe valk togedder to taouwn, zee? Valking, talking ve can do. Vouat you Americanzay, eh? Vwe can . . . *havitall*!" He roared with laughter. "You vill luv ztory. Juzt like *Arraby Nightz!*" He wiggled his suet suggestively. Father looked besieged. "Here goez!" As we made our way toward the bridge, Popov tweaked Father's ear with affection.

"A prracticionerr general," Popov began, "a Frrenchi name ov *Tourte*—zuch zilly name for *un docteur, n'ezt pas?*" He wrinkled his nose and pursed his lips to make himself look like an uptight French professional, "ina beeg Italian haouze: putti here, putti zere—" With Father on his arm, he danced to the left, then to the right. "And waz happy. Married to Oh! Ah! Baoutiful lady. Maybe you zee her Grroppi!" He dropped Father's arm to give us a demonstration of the lady's curves in the air.

"This is horrible, Liz!" Father managed to whisper in my ear as Popov was going on about caviar, class, and smoked fish:

"Za *wourks*! She: tazty dizsh!" He veered back and reached for Father's arm again, but Father recoiled, folding his arms across his chest.

"But da *docteur* iz grreedy! One by one he vizit all"—he turned to me—"I can zay voird *vhore* in front ov girli?"

"Now, *hold on*!" Father said. "You stop this, Boris!"

"Ah! Oh! *Come on,* profezzor!" Popov pleaded. "Vatz a vhore you tell me? Peoplez. Like any peoplez." He looked at Father with distrust. "You no *mizogynizt*?"

"Of course not!"

"Good!" Pleased, Popov smiled. "Lady," he continued, rocking on his rubber soles, "out herr mind *ennui.* Vunday—sheer accident! She make acquaintance Madam maybe in *hammán* and *Bam!* Friends already! *Bam!*" He clapped his hands.

"Stop!" Father screamed. "*Cessez vos idioties, Monsieur.* I will not allow you, I *forbid* you, to serve up any more of your vomitous goose, hot or cold: *je n'en veux pas!* You have no right," he approached Popov wagging a finger, "to taunt me!"

In preparation for a scuffle, Popov pulled off his spectacles and dropped them into the pocket of his shirt.

"Don't you think I know exactly what you are about?" Father cried, "Telling a coarse, smutty, a, a ludicrous and loathsome story! Taunting me with your veiled references and this, and this . . . *devant ma fille!*" Again he put his arm protectively around me. "You are no better than a pimp! Yes! You heard me, Popov! A pimp! A pimp!"

"Story?" I wondered. What story? *What was the story?*

"Vouat you suggest?" Popov stammered, foam spattering his mouth. He retrieved his glasses and put them on. "You arre mad! *Fou! Fou! Fou!*" he spat. *"Un grand fou!"* Like a piece of beef hurled onto a butcher's block, Popov slammed off in a huff.

We were near the bridge and began to make our way across. Father had been so exhausted by what had transpired I could see his skull peeping out from under the flesh of his face. I felt a deep sorrow for him, but also an irrepressible impatience.

"I know," Father whispered, his eyes swimming with tears, "she sleeps around."

"How do you know that?" I cried.

He said:

"Because she always has." In the light of the lamps people passed; a few gazed at us with curiosity.

"Only a monster," Father panted, "would inflict such pain." Did he mean Popov or Mother? I took his hand. For a long time we walked in silence, a renewed tenderness between us.

Already we were on Opera Square as if spirited there, approaching the lovely old Maydan Opera House that would burn down twenty years later and be replaced by a car park. Orchestra music from the Continental Savoy Hotel and the sounds of a brass band in the Ezbekièh Gardens flooded the streets. Gasping for breath, Father said:

"*Il faut partir.* There is nothing to be done. I shall tell the university tomorrow. I could not survive another year. I cannot bear this"—with his free hand he designated the men in throngs who filled the square—"any longer."

Unsummoned, a cab pulled up beside us. Shouting our address, Father threw himself inside, dragging me after. As if for an emergency the driver tore off, pounding his horn with his fist. He drove dangerously close to the sidewalk where elegant couples stood, impatient to cross over and join the dancing in the hotel's gleaming ballroom. At the corner of al-Gumhuriya and 26 Juillet, we saw Mother. Wearing a white sequined dress, she radiated light. As the cab turned, Father and I looked again to see if this were, indeed, she, not just another "symbolic manifestation," one of the many look-alikes she had spawned. We were so close we might have touched her.

With a fluid gesture, her companion tugged her out of harm's way and leaned into her neck. Mother threw back her head and laughed as he kissed her beneath her ear. It was he; of course it was he! As we passed them in the flickering of night, she mouthed his name: *Ram.* Trussed up like a leg of lamb, I sat immobilized in the shadows.

I recall how the next day when Ramses Ragab came to play at war (the Polish forces were to confront Teutonic knights on the field of Grünewald) Beybars refused to open the door, shouting, as if to a beggar: *Imshee! Imshee!* Ramses Ragab called out for Father who, surrounded by Polish horses, held his hands over his ears like a child. How hard the world is on a man who does not know how to cease being a child!

That evening Mother came. This time Beybars opened the door. She stood on the threshold to my room as Beybars, uneasy, hovered nearby and as Father pretended to paint a horse. When I refused to acknowledge her, she came into my room and reached for my wrist. She tried to pull me up from my bed where I was stubbornly reading. I bit her hard, in the soft place between her finger and thumb. I bit her savagely. Only when she was reeling with rage and pain did I look into her face. I felt like a heavy stone, a statue of salt; I could not move but only stare as she backed away cursing me before fleeing. After she had gone I sat tasting her blood. It seemed my heart had split in two and that blood was flooding my mouth. Although I did not see him, I knew Father was poised above a tiny horse and that the paint on his brush was drying. The brush would be ruined, and he would have to throw it away.

When I moved it was to pick up a needle from the small vortex of my dresser and to thrust it, again and again, into the center of the glyph on my wrist; to, in this way, harm all of us, punish each and every one of us. I did this until the pain was intolerable. Then I cried out for Father who held me for a very long time. Still Beybars remained standing in the hall. Only when in the kitchen a pan began to scorch did he hasten away. A stew of meat had burned, and our eyes stung with smoke. Scowling Beybars opened all the windows.

———

It was in the days before our departure that Father began his book on absolute monarchies and other societies dominated and assured by the power of the army. The writing of the initial notes for the book, and the tedious job of packing thousands of soldiers in tissue paper, appeared to occupy his mind entirely. Meanwhile Beybars cared for my wound—it had become badly infected—and healed it with a paste of leaves and petals. This is how I remember Beybars best: standing at my bedside with a box of simples in his hand.

On our last night in Cairo, after Beybars had gone home and Father had fallen asleep, someone knocked gently at our front door. As quietly as I could, I walked down the hall and pressed my cheek against it. The door felt warm and smooth; it felt like skin. After a time I heard Ramses Ragab say my name.

Breathless with pain, barely able to speak, I said:

"You were Father's friend." My bitterness so great it needled my tongue, I waited many long minutes to hear what he would say.

"The mistake I made," he said softly, "was to love the three of you." His words so confused me that I stood, my cheek to the door, unable to respond. After a time I could tell that he had gone. The next day Father and I boarded the ship that would take us back to America, West Wilbur, New Hampshire, and the age of Senator McCarthy.

FOURTEEN

Battles at Sea

Hathor, the goddess of revelry and love, oversees the City of the Dead. Here the departed dwell in erotic anticipation. Desire flourishes in painted rooms where the dead are invited to celebrate the world among the living. Here sowing and harvest are simultaneous, as are the feast and the hunt. The goose, trussed and ready for the oven, is roasted, set out on the table, reconfiguring itself as it is eaten, already hiding among the fragrant rushes. How the fragrance of goose, of rushes fills the nostrils! And just as the wine is poured into the cup, the grapes are crushed and all the while—how quickly pass the seasons!—the blind harpist never ceases to play. A flock of birds flies across the moon with a clatter, a bouquet of blue lotus is lovingly gathered, lovingly offered; the bread is brought to the table steaming; the harpist is sighted; the new wine tasted. If you look into your cup—and it is bottomless—you may read the words:

Death is rectifiable.

The departed is everywhere. He haunts his beloved, pressing upon her on all sides: sitting on a chair gazing at his own heart, slaying three or four crocodiles, playing at draughts, adoring the lion-gods of yesterday and today. Sailing on a river teeming with fishes, the sky above reeling with stars. Such profusion! He can barely make way. The reeling air, the teeming water contain him as in a net. Yet how beautiful he is, on the verge of resurgency, scooping up water with his hands. He, the departed, Lord of hearts, slayer of the heart, more elusive than the stars! Later she will awaken in the middle of the night quickened by the impossibility that he has only just left the room. Yet . . . what of the hawk wheeling and wheeling over her house? The owl calling in solitude? The sky bright with promise? Surely he is close by.

She implores Hathor, so distant on her moon:

> May he have an abundance of water!
> May he remember how to breathe the air!
> May he come forth from yesterday!
> May he remember his name!

The cup, placed on the altar, tastes of salt. A thousand years will pass, a thousand more. See how the wine, the tears, have left no trace in this perfect cup of alabaster, a cup as thin, as translucent, as the shells Hathor once tossed from the moon. Yet one should not, must not, revere such things. They bleed the present of vitality. Longing for what is lost, one enters a painted room where beauty is static and nothing anticipated because everything has already happened. As when Father in convalescence puts his bright soldiers down upon the counterpane and forgets that time is brittle, has broken, and cannot be mended. As when I, on a distant afternoon, take up my dolls and do not notice when evening has ambushed the room.

———

This talk of dolls causes me to recall that Popov was said to own a doll the size of a small-boned woman; her long black hair had once swept flies from the rump of a horse. It was Beybars who told me about her one subterranean afternoon as I watched him pluck a bird.

Beybars told me she had been made to order by a slipper maker. Cleverly articulated, even her lips could be opened. Her teeth were of elephant ivory—in those days so many things were made of ivory, even the Sporting Club's swizzle sticks!—and she had a tongue of red leather.

"And her eyes?" I had asked. "Are they of ivory, too?"

"Ah, no." Beybars whispered, closing his own eyes and touching the lids with the fingers of both his hands. "They are made of blue glass." He drummed the lids of his eyes lightly with his fingers.

"The Russian is repellent," Beybars pronounced with ferocity. "He is a pagan and an atheist." I nodded, although still close enough to girlhood to recall my own dolls with nostalgia. Yet I could not dare imagine why a grown man, as bristled as a sow, and a scholar, would want to own such a thing.

"The Russian is repellent," Beybars repeated. "It is good, very good, he comes here no more." I knew he was thinking not only of Popov but of Ramses Ragab and Mother when he added: "Praise God. This is a *clean* house."

I asked for more details about Popov's doll. Beybars told me that her beauty was a pretext, merely, to *awaken all the senses*. The leather of her body had been rubbed to a softness; she had been scented with jasmine; sewn within her chest beneath her breasts a little box made a sound like sighing when pressed; a honey drop was tucked beneath her tongue.

"The senses are entrapment!" Beybars spoke with conviction. "It is as the magician said."

Her name was Koot-el-Kuloob. Koot-el-Kuloob! I recognized her as the heroine of the tale called "The Fisherman and the River Apes." It troubled me that Popov read *The Arabian Nights*. Koot-el-Kuloob! So, Popov, too, dreamed of love in rooms with walls of sandalwood, studded with silver stars! Popov, too, loved reading of brass horsemen and speaking apes, of pillars of black stone and the islands of Wák-Wák, of feasts of jam served on plates of red gold.

"A silly name." Beybars shook his head in disbelief. "The whole affair smells of infidelity and whimsy."

"Do you suppose he *speaks to her*?" I blurted, deeply agitated.

"She has little ears," Beybars whispered, pulling the lobe of his own left ear, "sewn, begging your pardon, from the testicle leather of a lamb. Surely this is proof enough he speaks to her. Only the devil knows what she hears. If I had the power," Beybars said with seriousness, "to put fools into bottles of brass, so I would *bottle that Popov*!" I laughed then, imagining Popov in a thousand years released from his bottle and in a puff of blue smoke calling out, the top of his head combing the clouds: "Is not just creepsi, da?"

Beybars, recovering his usual good humor, laughed too.

"You are right to laugh at human folly." He smiled at me with real affection. "And I should not be so angry at the lonely man—so ugly too! A man who cannot find himself a real bride of flesh and bones! At least he can count on her constancy," he muttered to himself, but loud enough for me to hear.

I, too, wished to share a story of Popov with Beybars:

Earlier in the summer, Father and I were in the museum together looking at a little wooden boat. The cabin, in the shape of a shrine, contained miniature ceramic dishes of fish and fruit and flowers. It was guarded by a big-bellied dwarf in a comical wig. When we heard someone sneeze and saw Popov at the other end of the room—Popov whose jocular violence had already come to burden Father's precarious existence—we ducked behind a colossal cow and held hands as, trumpeting into his handkerchief,

Popov passed within a foot of us. When we thought we were safe, we made our way to Room 86 where Tut's board games were on display, his little boxes of cosmetics, his mirrors. Suddenly Popov poked his head round the door. He sneezed again; we slipped behind a colossal pink granite hippopotamus and, when we could, smuggled ourselves out of the museum and into the street where we fell into each other's arms laughing. I had not seen Father laugh in ages and it sobered me to think how much had been taken from him—Father who, unable to inspire it, had always craved what he had come to call "meatballs and the moon": domestic tenderness.

All at once jubilant Father cried: "Let's see if the chess set has been repaired!" We set off, took a wrong street, then another. Lost, we wandered the sumptuous, smoky squalor of the glass-makers' quarter, lingered among improbable dentists and plausible barbers; were distracted by incalculable fly swatters, dog whips, brass beds, striped mattresses, lemonade sellers, and trays of figs. When we found the ivory carver's shop at last and learned that the chess set would be ready within the week, we celebrated at a shaky table draped in a pristine, if much mended, cloth.

"What did you eat?" asked Beybars.

"Hot bowls of *ful*!"

"Bah!" Beybars shook his head. "Why eat beans when you can eat pomegranates?"

"The beans were wonderful," I told him. "And we were happy. Totally pleased with our lives. *Mabsoot!*"

A few weeks before our departure, Father's and mine, Beybars told me that Popov had torn Koot-el-Kuloob apart, torn out her tongue, torn off her eyes of blue glass and her little ears. Out of his mind with remorse, he had carried the doll's shattered body to the slipper maker for repair, holding, in a trembling hand, the smashed box that once contained her faithless sighs.

"The slipper maker threw him out!" Beybars clapped his hands with satisfaction. "The living alone know virtue."

———

We sailed home, Father and I, from Alexandria on a new Italian ship named the *Domenica da Paradiso.* The very first night of our journey, Father found a companion at chess. Father was entirely ethereal now; the chess alone grounded him. He played with intensity and flair, some said genius, and quickly became a celebrity. He claimed a small table in the ship's library; the magnetized game was left out between rounds. No one ever touched a piece; the little table served as a sacred space. Passengers were superstitious about it, whispering the *Domenica da Paradiso* could not sink as long as Father was at chess.

Father played with such fever, such "genial perversity" (in the words of an admirer), the initial games were dispatched with alacrity: before we were out forty-eight hours Father had humiliated twelve players. When an Italian novelist with the wonderful name of Michelangelo Buonarroti held on and Father, the gap between his teeth in evidence, was submerged in a "deep game," I wandered the decks alone, at chess of another kind.

There were a number of teenagers on board who briefly attempted to befriend me. They were thin, almost to invisibility, unformed, giddy, and green. The boys smelled of egg. They were noisy, wanting attention. One walked on his hands whenever he saw me; he executed cartwheels. I ignored him.

I wanted a man. This thought thrilled and motivated me. I wanted *to show him every favor*—if yet unaware of this phrase's full significance. I wanted to *transport him* (another phrase gleaned from *The Arabian Nights*). I wanted to master *all the rituals of love.* I explored the ship, riddling over the border between the licit and the illicit in my mind, shamelessly carrying my intentions around like a lighted lantern. I snaked from place to place as when—and always after everyone was seated and starting on their soup—I crossed the dining room to join Father, already in eager conversation with our table mates: the del Machias, the lecherous and archaic Senor Guiducci, a very pink Miss Able Brink, the amiable Megallys, the bitter Henry Grass. Sooner or later the conversation always turned to chess.

In the Old Kingdom, reason was said to dwell in the heart, as did insight and perception. In my thinnest dress and three new bracelets of blue glass neatly disguising my bandaged wrist, I went forth by day, by night to weave my spells of uplifting, my spells of taking and having. I whored among the tables set like shrines with blossoms and meat, filling the air with my scent of attar (and grey amber—for this had been Mother's gift, the one chosen by Ramses Ragab. I could not help but hold on to it—one does not toss away, not even in anger, a thing so precious. The amber—and she had given me a generous piece, the size of the pit of a peach—made palpable a vanished world and its fables. I knew, because Ramses Ragab had told me, that the ancients believed grey amber was the excrement of a fabulous bird, or honey fallen into the tropical sea and congealed by the action of salt and the waves, or that it was the egg of the philosophers hatched by the power of sunlight. *So I shall smell of the shit of a fabled creature,* I thought as it melted, so slowly! in my hand. *I shall smell of honey . . .*).

I could tell I was causing a stir and more: a *commotion* among the men. My insightful, my perceptive, my reasonable heart was after refinement, a certain tone of voice, depth of eye; a certain ease of manner. If he shared an anatomical resemblance to Ramses Ragab; if he were dark and wore white linen suits, all the better. My heart did not give a damn if he: the gazelle man, the lion-headed man, the blue falcon, the personification of the burning heat of the sun, traveled with a female companion—mistress or wife. Already I had begun to trouble the hours of any number of men, knowing with growing astonishment and dark delight what Mother knew. I thought: *I will outdo her.*

Popov's intrusion into my secret garden had been brief. *The Arabian Nights,* its network of intrigues and uncontrollable dangers, its elaborate, emblematic sexuality, its inventories of infamy, ecstatic punishments, prophetic fevers, and mystical escapes; its fortunate fishermen and treacherous barber surgeons; its charlatans, beauties, hunchbacks, transfigurations; its lovers, their monstrous theatricality, their exemplary transparency—all this was mine again. Baroque, glassy, animated by sparks and shadows, the tales embraced and encouraged me.

I made my choice. I liked him for many reasons. He was Egyptian, he did not follow me around, he did not gaze at me from across the dining room with love-sick eyes, but with evident humor. Somehow he conveyed that *he knew what I was up to.* He read me and would not be duped. It was above all his tender irony that made him so attractive.

So: a mere moment of our hands barely touching as we passed each other at the end of dinner was all it took to win me. A moment that haunted me for a night and a day, a day when my heart thrashed like an eel under the net of his eyes. Then it was once more evening. Dinner over, people had moved to the ballroom to dance, or roost in the lounge. Father was at chess with Buonarroti, and I in a high, windy place above the intemperate sea, having brushed off a petty officer and the adolescent acrobat's ultimate advance.

"Your name is Elizabeth—" He was beside me, his voice low, briefly incorporeal. I listened without turning to face him.

"Your father calls you Lizzie; the entire ship knows this; your names crop up everywhere and I . . . what shall I call you?"

"Lizoo," I said, as if from a dream. Still I dared not look at him. For godsake, I thought, why *Lizoo*?

"It's time you stopped prowling the decks, Lizoo." He stood very close. "Your scent is in everyone's nostrils. The young beauties and their mothers are defeated, and the boys are all insomniacs." Stealing a glance at his marvelous face, I laughed.

"This is a plea for peace, Liz," he said. Gently he caressed the nape of my neck with his little finger. "It is a plea for pleasure." I stood as still as a cat. "What would you like to call me?" His finger traveled to my collarbone and then from my shoulder to the bangles on my wrist. He was tremendously clever. Had he attempted to kiss me, I would have bolted.

"Ram," I said.

"Ah!" he sighed, taking my hand in his own, the heat of his hand matching mine, exactly. "Ram is not one of my names." I laughed again.

"How many names do you have?"

"Too many," he said. "I come from a pretentious family. Who is *Ram*?"

"A gazelle." I faced him, feeling wild. He took my other hand. I held my breath and sucked my lower lip. I thought he was perfect. He smelled of verbena.

"Ah. And what am I, then?"

"You're one, too." I was astonishing myself.

"So . . ." he mused. "We're in mythical lands, now." He paused. "Nevertheless. Why don't you call me Nabil? It is, in fact, my name." We stood beneath great black patches of sky and, just barely, a moon.

"What animal am I, Nabil?" Aroused, I stretched, feeling beautiful.

"No animal," he said, winning me over again. Suddenly cautious he asked: "How old are you?"

"Fifteen," I lied. He said:

"So young!"

"It's good for a girl to be with a man," I offered at random, unsure if this were so.

"A precocious animal," he decided. His eyes like jewels, he eased me to him as the moon and all things dissolved in salt and fog. We were on our knees, needing protection from the wind yet somehow unaware: our interest in each other was acute. He kissed me again and again, and we had escaped death and had no knowledge of impending affliction. You see: I know what it is to be perfectly lost. Nabil and I made lovely, inarticulate sounds as we bedded down in wind and the deep throbbing of the ship's motors. Nabil kissed me, as methodical as stars, opening a way for himself to me: a royal road. I was lucky. Nabil was of such generous goodness! So why, knowing this, did I vacillate? And begin to slip away? Had I been so blunted by betrayal, or by some trick of nature that I could not remain with Nabil in the joyous place he had, with grace, offered?

I attempted to dislodge whatever it was that had begun to feed upon me and pitched from side to side. But it persisted; no longer on the creep, it pounced. I slammed my head on the deck, certain I needed to be shattered in order to be reconfigured. And I needed to be reconfigured to be worthy of this man: Nabil.

Nabil stilled, held my head in his hands, attempted to pull away from me, but I held him close.

"It is cold here," he realized. "Shall we go down to my cabin? Surely you're cold."

"No," I protested, hiding my eyes from him.

"You are so restless," he murmured. "What is it you say in America? Settle down?" I laughed. A novice at sexual duplicity, nonetheless I moaned and stilled. Not that I was lying, exactly. I was begging the wind and the moon to give back what was being stolen and quickly, before an unbreachable rift came between me and pleasure. I needed Nabil to perform a wonder, surgery of the heart or necromancy, to keep me from sailing directly into the something gone missing that steadily claimed me. Instead, a mask tumbled to my face from the sky. A mask that would not begin to crack until years later when I would fall in love with Saleh. Yet, even then it did not crack quickly enough. High time it fell away. High time I tore it away! While I am still wanting the world. Before I, too, am sand and ashes!

———

Like an empty cup set out in a tomb, an old Polaroid of Saleh—how old is it now? twenty years? is the cipher for the sum of my losses. People say time sweeps everything away, but I know time is not the enemy, but sorrow. An empty cup is my constant sorrow—deeper than pain, deeper than pleasure, deeper, even, than time. I would fill it with sympathies!

When we lived together, Saleh and I, I once dreamed I was made of stones, stone upon stone heaped together. Saleh uttered a cry, like that of a hawk, and I fell down and was scattered.

Awaking, I described this dream to him. Tracing the bones of my face with his finger, Saleh sang an ancient Arabian song that begins with the lines:

> Fire is colder than the flames of my longing,
>   and stone softer than my lover's heart.
>   Her nature causes wonder:
>   a heart of stone in a body of water.

Then he kissed me, and with his usual delicacy, opened me with his fingers and I became water beneath his hands. I could not have articulated it then as I can now, but like Nabil, Saleh held the key to Schéhérazade's own sultry country. The burning key that, like a magnet, attracts, accumulates, and nourishes the world's heat. It is the same heat that causes the roses to deeply root and to blossom, the roses of Fayum that go into the making of the precious thing called "attar." That most precious thing that Ramses Ragab once had the thoughtfulness, the *sightedness* of heart, to give me. Long ago when I was still too young, too harmed, to comprehend its full significance.

I have been writing all winter. This morning, with my customary care, I broke apart a body that until that moment had been traveling undisturbed through time. Its eyes were fixed upon an absence I all too easily recognized. I held a pair of scissors and a razor—both very sharp; with these I lifted the flesh from the bones where it lay in long flakes—like the sails of a ship secured for the night. I recalled that even if his body had crumbled to dust, the departed awakens the instant Horus speaks his name. Then Horus quickens him with spells and "glorifications." With shame I realized I did not know the words for these. That I had never learned them. Carefully I cleaned my surgeon's tools and put them away.

In the Egypt of Old Time, the gods were in sympathy with the trees, presiding over their virtues and vitality. In this way a shady street is no different from a sacred grove or a temple garden.

When I left the museum the day was of severe brightness. The sun hung like a copper mirror in the sky, and I walked toward the acacias gratefully. Their scent was intoxicating, and I thought how even now the roses of Fayum are sublimated, how nothing is more essential to living in the world than transformation.

Acknowledgments

My thanks to Amy England, dearest friend, for her struggles with my handwriting and her clear-sightedness; to Michael du Plessis and Kathleen Chapman for the precious gift of necessary books; to Brian Kitely for the loan of his Cairo library; to Bradford Morrow for publishing chapters one, two, and six in *Conjunctions;* to Herbert Leibowitz for publishing an early version of chapter three in *Parnassus;* and to Jonathan, always and above all, *for listening.*

A NOTE ON THE TYPE

This book was set in Adobe Garamond. Designed for the Adobe Corporation by Robert Slimbach, the fonts are based on types first cut by Claude Garamond (c. 1480–1561). Garamond was a pupil of Geoffroy Tory and is believed to have followed the Venetian models, although he introduced a number of important differences, and it is to him that we owe the letter we now know as "old style." He gave to his letters a certain elegance and feeling of movement that won their creator an immediate reputation and the patronage of Francis I of France.

Composed by North Market Street Graphics
Lancaster, Pennsylvania

Printed and bound by R. R. Donnelley & Sons
Crawfordsville, Virginia

Designed by Soonyoung Kwon